D1215463

STAR TREK®

MOTION PICTURE TRILOGY

STAR TREK II: THE WRATH OF KHAN

ADAPTATION BY
ANDY SCHMIDT

SCREENPLAY BY
JACK B. SOWARDS

STORY BY
HARVE BENNETT AND JACK B. SOWARDS

ART BY
CHEE YANG ONG

COLORING BY
MOOSE BAUMANN

LETTERING BY
NEIL UYETAKE AND ROBBIE ROBBINS

EDITS BY
CHRIS RYALL AND SCOTT DUNBIER

STAR TREK III: THE SEARCH FOR SPOCK

ADAPTATION BY
MIKE W. BARR

SCREENPLAY BY
HARVE BENNETT

ART BY
TOM SUTTON, RIC ESTRADA, AND RICARDO VILLAGRAN

LETTERING BY
JOHN COSTANZA

COLORING BY
MICHELLE WOLFMAN

EDITS BY
MARV WOLFMAN

STAR TREK IV: THE VOYAGE HOME

ADAPTATION BY
MIKE W. BARR

SCREENPLAY BY
STEVE MEERSON & PETER KRIKES AND HARVE BENNETT & NICHOLAS MEYER

STORY BY
LEONARD NIMOY & HARVE BENNETT

ART BY
TOM SUTTON AND RICARDO VILLAGRAN

LETTERING BY
AGUSTIN MAS

COLORING BY
MICHELLE WOLFMAN

EDITS BY
ROBERT GREENBERGER

STAR TREK MOTION PICTURE TRILOGY

Collection edits by
JUSTIN EISINGER

Collection design by
NEIL UYETAKE

Cover by
CHEE YANG ONG

Cover colors by
MOOSE BAUMANN
assisted by Jennifer Baumann

Re-mastered and re-colored by
DIGIKORE STUDIOS LIMITED

Based on "Star Trek" created by
GENE RODDENBERRY

STAR TREK® II
THE WRATH OF KHAN

IN THE 23RD CENTURY...

CAPTAIN'S LOG:
STARDATE: 8130.3.
STARSHIP *ENTERPRISE* ON TRAINING MISSION TO GAMMA HYDRA. APPROACHING NEUTRAL ZONE.
MISTER SULU, PLOT A COURSE TO AVOID THE NEUTRAL ZONE.
AYE, CAPTAIN.
—IMPERATIVE! THIS IS THE KOBAYASHI MARU. -*SKAWK*- A GRAVITIC MINE -*SKAAK*- LOST POWER. -*SKWAAK*-
THIS IS THE STARSHIP *ENTERPRISE*. CAN YOU GIVE US YOUR COORDINATES?
-*SKKAKKT*- OUR POSITION IS GAMMA HYDRA, SECTION TEN -*SKWAAAK-AAAK*- LIFE SUPPORT FAILING. CAN YOU ASSIST US, *ENTERPRISE*?
THAT'S INSIDE THE NEUTRAL ZONE, CAPTAIN.
ENTERING THE NEUTRAL ZONE.
WE ARE NOW IN VIOLATION OF THE TREATY, CAPTAIN.
STAND BY TRANSPORTER ROOM. READY TO BEAM SURVIVORS ABOARD.

CAPTAIN! I'M GETTING SOMETHING ON THE DISTRESS CHANNEL.
ON SPEAKERS.

DAMN.
MISTER SULU? PLOT AN INTERCEPT COURSE.

CAPTAIN SAAVIK, MAY I REMIND YOU THAT ANY STARSHIP THAT ENTERS THE NEUTRAL ZONE IS IN VIOLATION—
THERE ARE OVER 300 PEOPLE ABOARD THAT SHIP. WE'RE GOING IN.

ALERT! THREE KLINGON CRUISERS CLOSING FAST.
VISUAL!

BATTLE STATIONS! RAISE SHIELDS!
EVASIVE ACTION!

SULU, GET US OUT OF HERE!
THOOM
FIRE ALL PHASERS!
THOOM
THOOM
THOOM

ALL HANDS, ABANDON SHIP...
ALL RIGHT, OPEN HER UP...
ANY SUGGESTIONS, ADMIRAL?
PRAYER, MISTER SAAVIK.
THE KLINGONS DON'T TAKE PRISONERS.

SPOCK? *AREN'T YOU DEAD?*
TRAINEES, TO THE BRIEFING ROOM.
PHYSICIAN, HEAL THYSELF.
IS THAT ALL YOU'VE GOT TO SAY? WHAT ABOUT MY PERFORMANCE?
I'M NOT A DRAMA CRITIC.
PERMISSION TO SPEAK CANDIDLY, SIR?
GRANTED.
I DON'T BELIEVE THIS WAS A FAIR TEST OF MY COMMAND ABILITIES. THERE WAS NO WAY TO WIN.
A NO-WIN SITUATION IS A POSSIBILITY EVERY COMMANDER MAY FACE. HAS THAT NEVER OCCURRED TO YOU?
NO, SIR. IT HAS NOT.

HOW WE DEAL WITH DEATH IS AT LEAST AS IMPORTANT AS HOW WE DEAL WITH LIFE.

THAT HAD NOT OCCURRED TO ME.
NOW YOU HAVE SOMETHING NEW TO THINK ABOUT.
CARRY ON.
ADMIRAL?

WOULDN'T IT BE EASIER TO JUST PUT AN EXPERIENCED CREW BACK ON THE SHIP?

GALLOPING AROUND THE COSMOS IS A GAME FOR THE YOUNG, DOCTOR.

NOW WHAT IS *THAT* SUPPOSED TO MEAN?

STARSHIP LOG. STARDATE 8130.4. LOG ENTRY BY FIRST OFFICER PAVEL CHEKOV.
STARSHIP RELIANT ON ORBITAL APPROACH TO CETI ALPHA SIX IN CONNECTION WITH PROJECT GENESIS.
WE ARE SEARCHING FOR A LIFELESS PLANET TO SATISFY THE REQUIREMENT OF A PROPER TEST SITE FOR GENESIS. BUT SO FAR...
...NO SUCCESS.
CAPTAIN, THIS PLANET IS NOTHING BUT DUST IN THE WIND. PERFECT FOR OUR TEST EXCEPT—
EXCEPT WHAT, COMMANDER?

CAPTAIN, DOES THE PLANET HAVE TO BE COMPLETELY LIFELESS?

DON'T TELL ME YOU FOUND SOMETHING DOWN THERE.

COME ON, LET'S CHECK IT OUT.
SEE IF IT'S SOMETHING WE CAN TRANSPLANT...

BING
BING

HAPPY BIRTHDAY, JIM!
ROMULAN ALE? WHY, BONES, YOU KNOW THIS IS ILLEGAL.

I ONLY USE IT FOR MEDICINAL PURPOSES. SPEAKING OF WHICH, THIS IS FOR YOU...
WHAT IS IT?
MORE ANTIQUES FOR YOUR COLLECTION. THEY'RE OVER 400 YEARS OLD.

THEY'RE FOR YOUR EYES. FOR MOST PATIENTS YOUR AGE I JUST PRESCRIBE RETINOX FIVE.
I'M ALLERGIC TO RETINOX FIVE.
EXACTLY.
NOW... CHEERS.

I DON'T KNOW WHAT TO SAY...

DAMMIT, JIM. OTHER PEOPLE HAVE BIRTHDAYS. WHY ARE WE TREATING YOURS LIKE A FUNERAL?
BONES, I DON'T WANT TO BE LECTURED.
THIS ISN'T ABOUT AGE. AND YOU KNOW IT.
IT'S ABOUT YOU FLYING A GODDAMN COMPUTER CONSOLE WHEN YOU WANT TO BE OUT THERE HOPPING GALAXIES!
WE ALL HAVE OUR ASSIGNED DUTIES.
DON'T. NOT WITH ME. YOU'RE HIDING.
WHO AM I HIDING FROM?
YOURSELF, ADMIRAL.
DON'T MINCE WORDS, BONES, WHAT DO YOU REALLY THINK?

JIM, I'M YOUR DOCTOR. I'M YOUR FRIEND.
GET BACK YOUR COMMAND.

CHEKOV, ARE YOU SURE THESE ARE THE RIGHT COORDINATES?
I CAN BARELY SEE ANYTHING.
THE TRICORDER MUST BE BROKEN.
...WAIT, I'M GETTING READINGS. OVER HERE.
YES, THERE'S SOMETHING...
...IT LOOKS LIKE CARGO CARRIERS.
BOTANY BAY. *BOTANY BAY?*
WE'VE GOT TO GET OUT OF HERE— *NOW!*
CHEKOV, WHAT'S THE MATTER WITH YOU?

YOU... I NEVER FORGET A FACE, MISTER... CHEKOV, ISN'T IT?
CHEKOV, WHO IS THIS MAN?

YOU MEAN TO TELL ME THAT HE NEVER TOLD YOU THE TALE?

HE NEVER TOLD YOU HOW THE ENTERPRISE PICKED UP THE BOTANY BAY, LOST IN SPACE FROM THE YEAR 1996?
I AM THE PRODUCT OF LATE 20TH CENTURY GENETIC ENGINEERING. AS IS MY CREW. WE WERE IN CRYOGENIC FREEZE.

WHAT YOU SEE IS ALL THAT REMAINS OF THE SHIP'S CREW...
...OF THE BOTANY BAY.
MAROONED HERE FIFTEEN YEARS AGO...

...BY CAPTAIN JAMES T. KIRK.

KHAN...

ADMIRAL KIRK?
ADMIRAL!
WE LEFT YOU ON A PLANET TEEMING WITH LIFE—CETI ALPHA FIVE WAS A PARADISE—

THIS IS CETI ALPHA FIVE!

CETI ALPHA SIX EXPLODED SIX MONTHS AFTER WE WERE LEFT HERE. THE SHOCK SHIFTED OUR ORBIT—THIS PLANET WAS LAID TO WASTE.
ADMIRAL KIRK NEVER BOTHERED TO CHECK ON OUR PROGRESS.

ON EARTH... 200 YEARS AGO... I WAS A PRINCE.

CHEKOV, YOU THOUGHT THIS WAS CETI ALPHA SIX... YOU DIDN'T EXPECT TO FIND ME HERE.
SO TELL ME, GENTLEMEN, IF NOT TO FIND US, THEN WHY ARE YOU HERE?

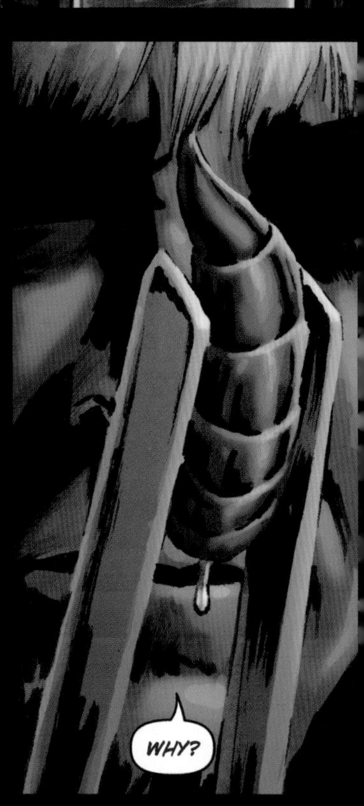
WHY?

I HATE INSPECTIONS.
I THINK YOU KNOW MY TRAINING CREW, ADMIRAL.
YES, WE'VE BEEN THROUGH DEATH... AND LIFE TOGETHER.
MR. SCOTT, YOU OLD SPACE DOG. YOU'RE WELL?
NO DUST, MR. SCOTT. WHAT A WELCOME SURPRISE ON THIS FLYING OLD DEATH TRAP.
OH, NO, SIR! THIS IS THE FINEST ENGINE ROOM IN THE WHOLE OF STARFLEET. IF THE ADMIRAL CAN'T SEE THE FACTS FOR HIMSELF...
...THEN HE'S AS BLIND AS A TIBERIAN BAT.
AND YOU ARE?
MIDSHIPMAN FIRST CLASS PETER PRESTON, ENGINEER'S FIRST MATE, SIR!
YOUR MIDSHIPMAN IS A TIGER.
MY SISTER'S YOUNGEST, ADMIRAL. CRAZY TO GET INTO SPACE.
WELL, MR. SCOTT, ARE YOUR ENGINES CAPABLE OF HANDLING A MINOR TRAINING CRUISE?
GIVE THE WORD, ADMIRAL.
MR. SCOTT...
...THE WORD IS GIVEN.

HE'S NEVER WHAT I EXPECT, SIR.
WHAT SURPRISES YOU, LIEUTENANT?
HE'S SO— HUMAN.
"NO ONE'S PERFECT, SAAVIK."
ADMIRAL ON THE BRIDGE.
RUNNING LIGHTS ON.

LIEUTENANT, HAVE YOU EVER PILOTED A STARSHIP OUT OF SPACE DOCK?
NEVER, SIR.

FOR EVERYTHING, THERE IS A FIRST TIME, LIEUTENANT. WOULDN'T YOU AGREE, ADMIRAL?

WOULD YOU LIKE A TRANQUILIZER?

"TAKE HER OUT, MR. SAAVIK."

SPACE STATION REGULA ONE.

LIEUTENANT, ARE YOU WEARING YOUR HAIR DIFFERENTLY?
IT'S STILL REGULATION.
MAY I SPEAK, SIR?

YOU'RE BOTHERED BY YOUR PERFORMANCE ON THE KOBYASHI MARU.
I FAILED TO RESOLVE THE SITUATION. MAY I ASK HOW YOU DEALT WITH THE TEST?
YOU MAY ASK...

THAT'S A LITTLE JOKE.

HUMOR.
HM.
ADMIRAL KIRK, WE HAVE AN URGENT MESSAGE COMING FROM DOCTOR CAROL MARCUS ON REGULA ONE.
THANK YOU, UHURA.

IT NEVER RAINS BUT IT POURS...
BONES, AS A PHYSICIAN, YOU OF ALL PEOPLE SHOULD APPRECIATE THE DANGERS...

...OF REOPENING OLD WOUNDS.

JIM, WHY ARE YOU TAKING GENESIS AWAY FROM US? WHO GAVE THE ORDER?
TAKING GENESIS? WHO IS? **WHO IS TAKING GENESIS?**
WHAT ORDER?
ON WHOSE AUTHORITY CAN THEY DO THIS?
WHOSE AUTHORITY?
NO ONE'S AUTHORITY!
PLEASE HELP US, JIM! WE'RE— **SQUAAK!**

CAROL?
CAROL!
UHURA! WHAT'S HAPPENING?
TRANSMISSION JAMMED AT THE SOURCE, SIR.

WE MUST HAVE ORDER HERE!
THIS MUST BE SOME SORT OF MISTAKE.
MISTAKE? WE'RE ALL ALONE HERE. THEY WAITED UNTIL EVERYONE WAS ON LEAVE TO STEAL GENESIS.
SCIENTISTS HAVE ALWAYS BEEN PAWNS FOR THE MILITARY—
I WON'T SUBSCRIBE TO YOUR INTERPRETATION OF EVENTS, DAVID.

EVEN SO, RELIANT IS ON HER WAY.

EVERYONE...
...GET YOUR GEAR TOGETHER.

WE HAVE A PROBLEM, SPOCK. SOMETHING MAY BE WRONG AT REGULA ONE. WE'VE BEEN ORDERED TO INVESTIGATE.
IF MEMORY SERVES, REGULA ONE IS A SCIENTIFIC RESEARCH LABORATORY.
I TOLD STARFLEET COMMAND ALL WE HAD WAS A BOATLOAD OF CHILDREN, BUT WE'RE THE ONLY SHIP IN THE QUADRANT.
SPOCK— THESE CADETS OF YOURS—HOW GOOD ARE THEY?
HOW WILL THEY RESPOND UNDER *REAL PRESSURE*?
LIKE ALL LIVING THINGS, EACH ACCORDING TO HIS GIFTS. OF COURSE...
...THE *SHIP IS YOURS*.
THAT WON'T BE NECESSARY.
IT MAY BE NOTHING. YOU TAKE THE SHIP.
JIM... YOU PROCEED FROM A FALSE ASSUMPTION. I AM A VULCAN.
I HAVE NO EGO TO BRUISE.

IF I MAY BE SO BOLD...
IT WAS A **MISTAKE** FOR YOU TO ACCEPT PROMOTION.
COMMANDING A STARSHIP IS YOUR FIRST, **BEST** DESTINY.
I WOULD NOT PRESUME TO DEBATE YOU. YOU'RE ABOUT TO REMIND ME THAT LOGIC ALONE DICTATES YOUR ACTIONS AND DECISIONS.

I WOULD NOT REMIND YOU OF THAT WHICH YOU KNOW SO WELL.
IN ANY CASE, WERE I TO INVOKE LOGIC, LOGIC CLEARLY DICTATES THAT THE NEEDS OF THE MANY OUTWEIGH THE NEEDS OF THE FEW.
OR THE ONE.

YOU ARE MY SUPERIOR OFFICER. YOU ARE ALSO MY FRIEND...
I HAVE BEEN, AND ALWAYS SHALL BE, YOURS.

MISTER SULU! SET COURSE FOR REGULA ONE.
LAYING IN COURSE, ADMIRAL.
MISTER SCOTT?
AYE, SIR!
WE'LL BE GOING TO WARP SPEED.
AYE, SIR!
ENGAGE WARP ENGINES.
SAAVIK, PREPARE SPEAKERS.
THIS IS ADMIRAL KIRK. AN EMERGENCY SITUATION HAS ARISEN. AS OF NOW, I AM ASSUMING COMMAND OF THIS VESSEL.
IT COULD BE NOTHING. OR IT COULD BE DANGEROUS. STARFLEET FEARS THE LATTER.
I KNOW NONE OF YOU EXPECTED THIS. I'M GOING TO HAVE TO ASK YOU TO GROW UP A LITTLE BIT SOONER THAN YOU INTENDED.
AND FOR THAT...
...I'M SORRY.

ART BY CHEE YANG ONG

PROJECT GENESIS SUMMARY.
GENESIS: CLASSIFIED.
DOCTOR CAROL MARCUS.
YES.
WHAT EXACTLY IS GENESIS? TO PUT IT SIMPLY, GENESIS IS LIFE FROM LIFELESSNESS.
IT IS A PROCESS WHEREBY MOLECULAR STRUCTURE IS REORGANIZED AT A SUBATOMIC LEVEL INTO LIFE-GENERATING MATTER OR EQUAL MASS.

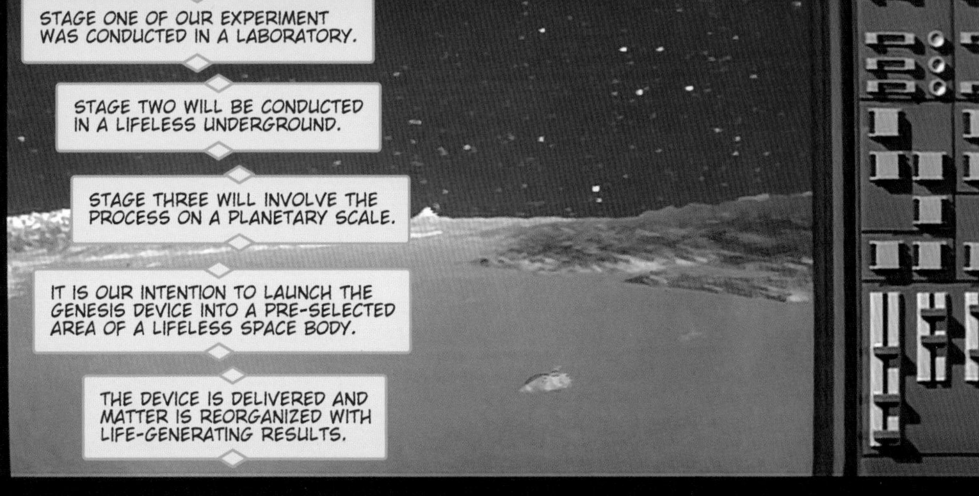
STAGE ONE OF OUR EXPERIMENT WAS CONDUCTED IN A LABORATORY.
STAGE TWO WILL BE CONDUCTED IN A LIFELESS UNDERGROUND.
STAGE THREE WILL INVOLVE THE PROCESS ON A PLANETARY SCALE.
IT IS OUR INTENTION TO LAUNCH THE GENESIS DEVICE INTO A PRE-SELECTED AREA OF A LIFELESS SPACE BODY.
THE DEVICE IS DELIVERED AND MATTER IS REORGANIZED WITH LIFE-GENERATING RESULTS.

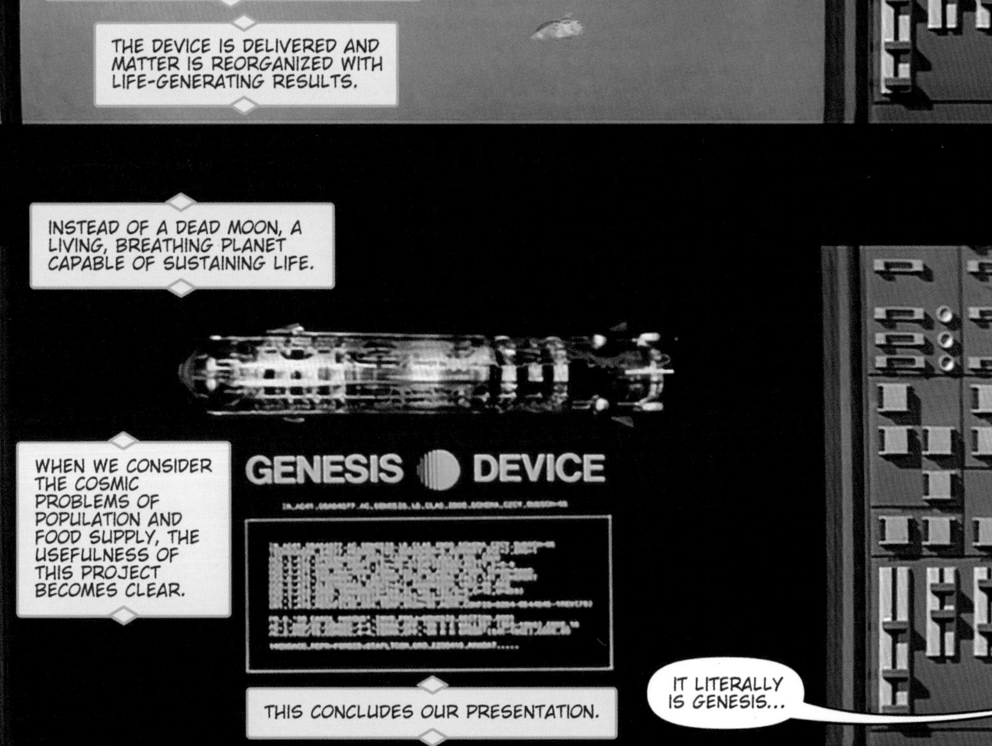
INSTEAD OF A DEAD MOON, A LIVING, BREATHING PLANET CAPABLE OF SUSTAINING LIFE.
WHEN WE CONSIDER THE COSMIC PROBLEMS OF POPULATION AND FOOD SUPPLY, THE USEFULNESS OF THIS PROJECT BECOMES CLEAR.
GENESIS DEVICE
THIS CONCLUDES OUR PRESENTATION.
IT LITERALLY IS GENESIS...

THIS PRESENTATION WAS GIVEN OVER A YEAR AGO, SPOCK. I CAN ONLY ASSUME IT'S ON TO STAGE TWO AT LEAST.
FASCINATING.
THAT'S WHAT THEY'RE WORKING ON AT REGULA ONE, CAPTAIN?
WHAT IF WE USED THIS THING WHERE LIFE ALREADY EXISTS?
IT WOULD DESTROY SUCH LIFE...
...IN FAVOR OF IT'S NEW MATRIX.
"IT'S NEW MATRIX." DO YOU HAVE ANY IDEA WHAT YOU'RE SAYING?
I WAS NOT ATTEMPTING TO EVALUATE ITS MORAL IMPLICATIONS, DOCTOR. AS A MATTER OF COSMIC HISTORY, IT HAS ALWAYS BEEN EASIER TO DESTROY THAN TO CREATE.
NOT ANYMORE! NOW WE CAN DO BOTH AT THE SAME TIME!
ACCORDING TO MYTH, THE EARTH WAS CREATED IN SIX DAYS. NOW WATCH OUT! ***HERE COMES GENESIS! WE CAN DO IT IN SIX MINUTES!***
ARE YOU BY ANY CHANCE IN FAVOR OF THESE EXPERIMENTS?
REALLY, DOCTOR MCCOY, YOU MUST LEARN TO GOVERN YOUR PASSIONS. LOGIC SUGGESTS—
MY GOD, THE MAN'S TALKING ABOUT LOGIC. WE'RE TALKING ABOUT ***UNIVERSAL ARMAGEDDON!***
GENTLEMEN, GENTLEMEN, THIS REALLY ISN'T THE PLACE—
BRIDGE TO ADMIRAL KIRK, WE HAVE A VESSEL CLOSING FAST— ***THE RELIANT***.

PICTURE, MR. SAAVIK.
AYE, CAPTAIN.

RELIANT IN OUR SECTION, ADMIRAL KIRK. MOVING ***SLOWLY***...
ACCORDING TO REGULATIONS, WHEN ANY VESSEL APPROACHES WITHOUT ESTABLISHED COMMUNICATION—
LIEUTENANT, THE ADMIRAL IS AWARE OF REGULATIONS.
IS IT POSSIBLE THEIR ***COMMS*** HAVE FAILED?
IT WOULD EXPLAIN A GREAT MANY THINGS...

THEY'RE REQUESTING COMMUNICATIONS. AND THEIR SHIELDS ARE STILL DOWN.
OF COURSE! WE ARE ONE BIG HAPPY ***FAMILY***.

AH, KIRK, MY OLD FRIEND. ARE YOU FAMILIAR WITH AN OLD KLINGON PROVERB THAT SAYS REVENGE IS A DISH...
...BEST SERVED COLD.
IT IS VERY COLD IN SPACE...

THIS IS DAMNED PECULIAR.
YELLOW ALERT.
ENERGIZE DEFENSE FIELDS.
THEY STILL HAVEN'T RAISED SHIELDS.
RAISE OURS.
THEY ARE ACTIVATING SHIELDS.
WH—
LOCK PHASERS.
RAISE SHIELDS!
FIRE!

BOOM

SULU, GET THOSE SHIELDS UP!
TRYING, SIR!
SCOTTY! THE WARP CORE ALARM!
BOOM BOOM
DEET DEET DEET DEET DEET DEET

AYE, SIR! SHE'S SPRUNG A LEAK!
CAN YOU FIX HER?
WITH A FEW MORE MEN...
DEET DEET DEET DEET DEET DEET DEET DEET DEET

DAMAGE REPORT.
THEY KNEW EXACTLY WHERE TO HIT US.
WHO HIT US?
AND *WHY*?
ONE THING IS CERTAIN. WE CANNOT ESCAPE ON AUXILIARY POWER.
DEET DEET DEET DEET DEET DEET DEET DEET DEET

WARP CORE PATCHED, ADMIRAL.
GOOD, SCOTTY.
THE MAIN ENERGIZER IS OUT. AUXILIARY POWER BACK IN A FEW MINUTES.
WE DON'T HAVE A FEW MINUTES!
PHASER POWER?
NOT ENOUGH AGAINST THEIR SHIELDS.

COMMANDER OF *RELIANT* SIGNALS, HE WISHES TO DISCUSS—
SIR, HE WISHES TO DISCUSS...
...TERMS OF OUR SURRENDER.

PUT HIM ON SCREEN.
SIR—
DO IT.
ON SCREEN.

KHAN...
YOU STILL REMEMBER ME, ADMIRAL.
I HAVE DEPRIVED YOUR SHIP OF POWER AND WHEN I SWING AROUND I INTEND TO DEPRIVE YOU OF YOUR LIFE.
GENESIS? WHAT'S THAT?
DON'T INSULT MY INTELLIGENCE, ADMIRAL.
GIVE ME TIME TO RECALL THE DATA.
I GIVE YOU... 60 SECONDS.
AT LEAST WE KNOW HE DOESN'T HAVE GENESIS.
KEEP NODDING AS THOUGH I'M GIVING ORDERS.
MR. SAAVIK, PUNCH UP THE DATA CHARTS ON THE *RELIANT* COMMAND CONSOLE.
THE PREFIX CODE?
IT'S ALL WE'VE GOT.

IF IT'S ME YOU WANT—
I WANTED YOU TO KNOW WHO IT WAS FIRST. ***WHO BEAT YOU***.
I'LL HAVE MYSELF BEAMED OVER TO YOU. SPARE MY CREW!

I OFFER A COUNTER PROPOSAL..

I'LL AGREE TO YOUR TERMS, IF—*IF*...
...IN ADDITION TO YOURSELF, YOU HAND OVER ALL MATERIALS ON—
—PROJECT GENESIS.

ADMIRAL.
WE'RE FINDING IT. YOU'VE GOT TO GIVE US TIME. THE BRIDGE IS SMASHED!

I DON'T UNDERSTAND...
YOU'VE GOT TO LEARN WHY THINGS WORK.
EACH STARSHIP IS EQUIPPED WITH ITS OWN PREFIX CODE TO PREVENT ENEMY SHIPS FROM DOING WHAT WE'RE ATTEMPTING.

YOU'RE USING OUR CONSOLE TO ORDER THE *RELIANT*...?
BIP BIP BIP BOOP BIP

MR. SULU. LOCK PHASERS.
PHASERS LOCKED.
TIME'S UP, ADMIRAL.
STAND BY TO RECEIVE OUR TRANSMISSION, KHAN.
NOW, MR. SPOCK.
SENDING...

BOOM

FIRE!

BOOM

SIR, OUR SHIELDS ARE FALLING.
WELL, RAISE THEM!
I CAN'T!
DOOP DOOP DOOP
FIRE.

FIRE!

BOOM

RETURN FIRE!
WE CAN'T! WE MUST WITHDRAW!
NO!

THE ENTERPRISE CAN WAIT, SIR!
SHE'S NOT GOING ANYWHERE!

SIR, YOU DID IT.
I DID NOTHING.
YOU GO RIGHT ON QUOTING REGULATIONS, MR. SAAVIK.
QUICKLY...

...LET'S SEE HOW BADLY—

MIDSHIPMAN PRESTON.
HE STAYED AT HIS POST.
WHEN THE TRAINEES A'RAN. HE STAYED AT HIS POST.

IS THE WORD GIVEN, ADMIRAL?

THE WORD IS GIVEN. WARP SPEED.

AYEEEHH—

I KNOW YOU TRIED, DOCTOR.
I'M SORRY, MISTER SCOTT.

ADMIRAL, WE'RE APPROACHING REGULA ONE.
DOCTOR McCOY. SAAVIK. YOU'RE WITH ME TO BEAM DOWN. SPOCK, YOU HAVE THE SHIP.
VERY WELL. BE CAREFUL, ADMIRAL.
WWWWWWMMMMM
I'M GETTING NO READINGS.
WAIT, LIFE SIGNS THIS WAY...
HERE!
CHEKOV!
WHAT HAPPENED TO THEM?

I'M NOT SURE YET.
UHHHHHH...
SIR, IT WAS KHAN... HE PUT CREATURES IN OUR EARS... TRIED TO CONTROL US... BUT HE...
...HE COULDN'T. WE BEAT HIM... THE CAPTAIN WAS STRONG...
CAPTAIN, WHERE IS DOCTOR MARCUS?
WHERE ARE THE GENESIS MATERIALS?
HE COULDN'T FIND THEM. EVEN THE DATABANKS WERE EMPTY.
HE MAROONED MY CREW ON CETI ALPHA FIVE.
HE TORTURED THE SCIENTISTS HERE, BUT NONE OF THEM WOULD TALK. HE WENT WILD... SLIT THEIR THROATS.
HE'S COMPLETELY MAD, ADMIRAL. HE BLAMES YOU FOR THE DEATH OF HIS WIFE.
I KNOW WHAT HE BLAMES ME FOR.

ESCAPE PODS ARE ALL IN PLACE...
WHERE'S THE TRANSPORTER ROOM?

KIRK TO ENTERPRISE. DAMAGE REPORT.
SPOCK HERE.
ADMIRAL, IF WE GO BY THE BOOK, LIKE LIEUTENANT SAAVIK, HOURS WOULD SEEM LIKE DAYS.
I READ YOU, CAPTAIN. LET'S HAVE IT.

"THEN THIS WILL BE YOUR BIG CHANCE TO GET AWAY FROM IT ALL..."
WWVVVVMMMMMM
FAN OUT.
ADMIRAL, LOOK.
GENESIS, I PRESUME.

YOU!

UNG!
WHUMP

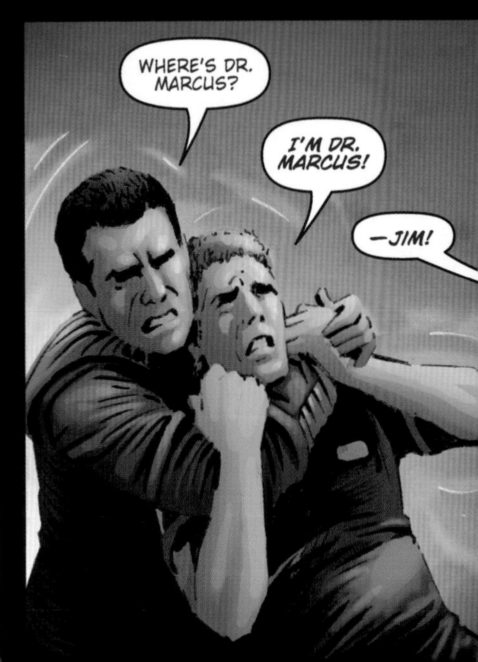
WHERE'S DR. MARCUS?
I'M DR. MARCUS!
—JIM!

CHEKOV?

YOUR EXCELLENCY, HAVE YOU BEEN LISTENING?
I HAVE INDEED...
SIR, YOU HAVE THE COORDINATES TO BEAM UP GENESIS.

VVVVVVVMMMMMMM

NOW KILL ADMIRAL KIRK.

MOTHER, HE KILLED EVERYONE WE LEFT BEHIND.
OF COURSE HE DIDN'T. DAVID, YOU'RE JUST MAKING THIS HARDER.

I'M AFRAID IT'S HARDER THAN YOU THINK, DOCTOR.
PLEASE DON'T MOVE.

SIR, IT IS DIFFICULT, I... I TRY TO OBEY.
KILL HIM!

THOSE THINGS ARE STILL IN THEIR BRAINS.
LET ME HELP YOU, MAN!

YOU CAN'T—
SHRAAK

CHEKOV, KILL HIM!
NOOAAAAAAWWWWW!
BLEEP BLEEP
BLEEP BLEEP BLEEP
KHAN, YOU BLOO SUCKER!
YOU'RE GOING TO HAVE TO DO YOUR OWN DIRTY WORK NOW. DO YOU HEAR ME?
DO YOU?
KIRK.
YOU'RE STILL ALIVE, OLD FRIEND.
STILL.
OLD.
FRIEND.

FOR GOD'S SAKES, WHAT IS IT?
SHRAAK
YOU'VE MANAGED TO KILL JUST ABOUT EVERYONE ELSE, BUT LIKE A POOR MARKSMAN, YOU KEEP MISSING THE TARGET.
I'VE DONE FAR WORSE THAN KILL YOU... I'VE HURT YOU. AND I WISH TO GO ON...
...HURTING YOU.
I SHALL LEAVE YOU AS YOU LEFT ME... AS YOU LEFT HER.
I WILL LEAVE YOU MAROONED IN THE CENTER OF A DEAD PLANET.
BURIED ALIVE.
KHAN!

100 MINUTES LATER...
THIS IS LIEUTENANT SAAVIK CALLING *ENTERPRISE*.
IT'S NO USE, ADMIRAL. THEY'RE STILL JAMMING OUR CHANNELS.
CHEKOV'S COMING AROUND.
IF THE ENTERPRISE IS FOLLOWING ORDERS, SHE'S LONG SINCE GONE. IF SHE DIDN'T OBEY, THEN SHE'S... ***FINISHED***.
SO ARE WE, IT LOOKS LIKE.

SIR, ABOUT THE KOBAYASHI MARU?
ARE YOU ASKING ME IF WE'RE PLAYING OUT THAT SCENARIO NOW?
WILL YOU TELL ME WHAT ***YOU*** DID? I'D REALLY ***LIKE*** TO KNOW.

LIEUTENANT, YOU ARE LOOKING AT THE ONLY STARFLEET CADET TO EVER BEAT THE "NO-WIN SCENARIO."
HOW?

I REPROGRAMMED THE SIMULATION SO IT WAS ***POSSIBLE*** TO RESCUE THE SHIP.
HE ***CHEATED***.
I ***CHANGED*** THE ***CONDITIONS*** OF THE TEST. ***I DON'T LIKE TO LOSE***.

THEN YOU'VE NEVER FACED THAT SITUATION—***FACED DEATH***.

RIGHT... IS THERE ANYTHING TO EAT? I'M STARVING.
THERE'S FOOD IN THE GENESIS CAVE. ENOUGH TO LAST A LIFETIME... IF NECESSARY.
WE THOUGHT THIS WAS GENESIS?

HARDLY. DAVID, WHY DON'T YOU SHOW DOCTOR McCOY AND THE LIEUTENANT OUR IDEA OF FOOD?
THIS IS JUST TO GIVE US SOMETHING TO DO, ISN'T IT?
COME ON. FOLLOW ME.

I DID WHAT YOU WANTED. I STAYED AWAY.
WHY DIDN'T YOU TELL HIM?

WERE WE TOGETHER? WERE WE *GOING* TO BE? YOU HAD YOUR LIFE AND I HAD MINE.
AND I WANTED HIM IN *MINE*.

HE'S A LOT LIKE YOU IN MANY WAYS.

PLEASE TELL ME WHAT YOU'RE FEELING.
THERE'S A MAN OUT THERE I HAVEN'T SEEN IN *FIFTEEN YEARS*. HE'S TRYING TO *KILL ME*. YOU SHOW ME A SON WHO'D BE *HAPPY* TO *HELP*.
MY *SON*... MY LIFE THAT COULD HAVE BEEN, BUT *WASN'T*.
WHAT AM I FEELING?
OLD. WORN OUT.

COME ON. LET ME SHOW YOU SOMETHING...

"...THAT WILL MAKE YOU FEEL YOUNG, LIKE WHEN THE WORLD WAS NEW."

YOU DID ALL THIS IN A DAY?
CAN I COOK OR CAN'T I?
KIRK TO SPOCK. IT'S BEEN TWO HOURS.
RIGHT ON TIME. WE'LL BEAM YOU UP.
HOW—?
MISTER SAAVIK, YOU OF ALL PEOPLE SHOULD KNOW REGULATION 46-A. "IF TRANSMISSIONS ARE BEING MONITORED DURING BATTLE—
"—NO UNCODED MESSAGES ON AN OPEN CHANNEL." BUT—
I DON'T LIKE TO LOSE.

ART BY CHEE YANG ONG

"ADMIRAL ON THE BRIDGE."
BATTLE STATIONS.
THERE ISN'T TIME TO EXPLAIN. SUFFICE IT TO SAY, KHAN—A MADMAN—HAS THE GENESIS DEVICE AND IS TRYING TO KILL US.
HE'S OUT THERE AND HE'S HUNTING US.
YOU'LL ALL DO YOUR LEVEL BEST, I HAVE NO DOUBT.
TACTICAL.
RELIANT CAN STILL OUTRUN US ***AND*** OUT GUN US.
BUT THERE IS THE MUTARA NEBULA AT HEADING ONE-FIVE-THREE-MARK-FOUR.
SIR, WE'LL BE BLIND AND IT WILL DISABLE OUR SHIELDS.
THE ODDS WILL BE ***EVEN***.

THERE SHE IS.
NOT SO WOUNDED AS WE WERE LED TO BELIEVE, IS SHE?
SO MUCH THE BETTER.
FOLLOW HER.

THE *RELIANT* IS CLOSING...

NAVIGATION, WHY ARE WE SLOWING?
IF THEY GO IN THERE, WE'LL LOSE THEM. OUR ***SHIELDS*** WILL BE ***USELESS!***

THE *RELIANT* IS SLOWING, ADMIRAL.
REMIND ME TO EXPLAIN TO YOU THE CONCEPT OF THE HUMAN EGO.
WHAT HAPPENS IF HE DOES NOT FOLLOW US INTO THE NEBULA, SIR?
PUT HIM ON SCREEN.

WE TRIED IT ONCE YOUR WAY, KHAN. ARE YOU GAME FOR A REMATCH?
KHAN...
...I'M ***LAUGHING*** AT THE SUPERIOR INTELLECT.

FULL IMPULSE POWER.
NO, SIR.
FULL POWER, DAMN YOU!

OFF SCREEN.
I'LL SAY THIS FOR HIM—
—HE'S CONSISTENT.
WE ARE NOW ENTERING THE MUTARA NEBULA.
PING

FZZT SKKT ZZZH

TACTICAL?
USELESS, SIR.
EMERGENCY LIGHTS.

SHIP TO SHIP, HE WILL BEAT US.
HE FOLLOWED ME THIS FAR...

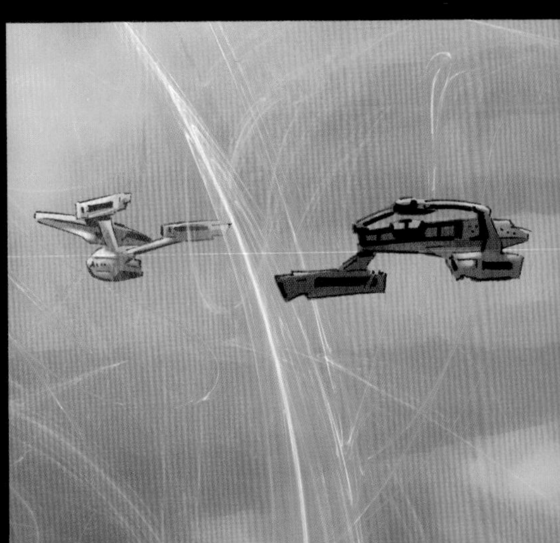

HOLD YOUR COURSE, MR. SULU.

HE'S INTELLIGENT BUT NOT EXPERIENCED...

HE'S NOT THINKING IN THREE DIMENSIONS...
...FULL STOP. LOAD TORPEDOES.

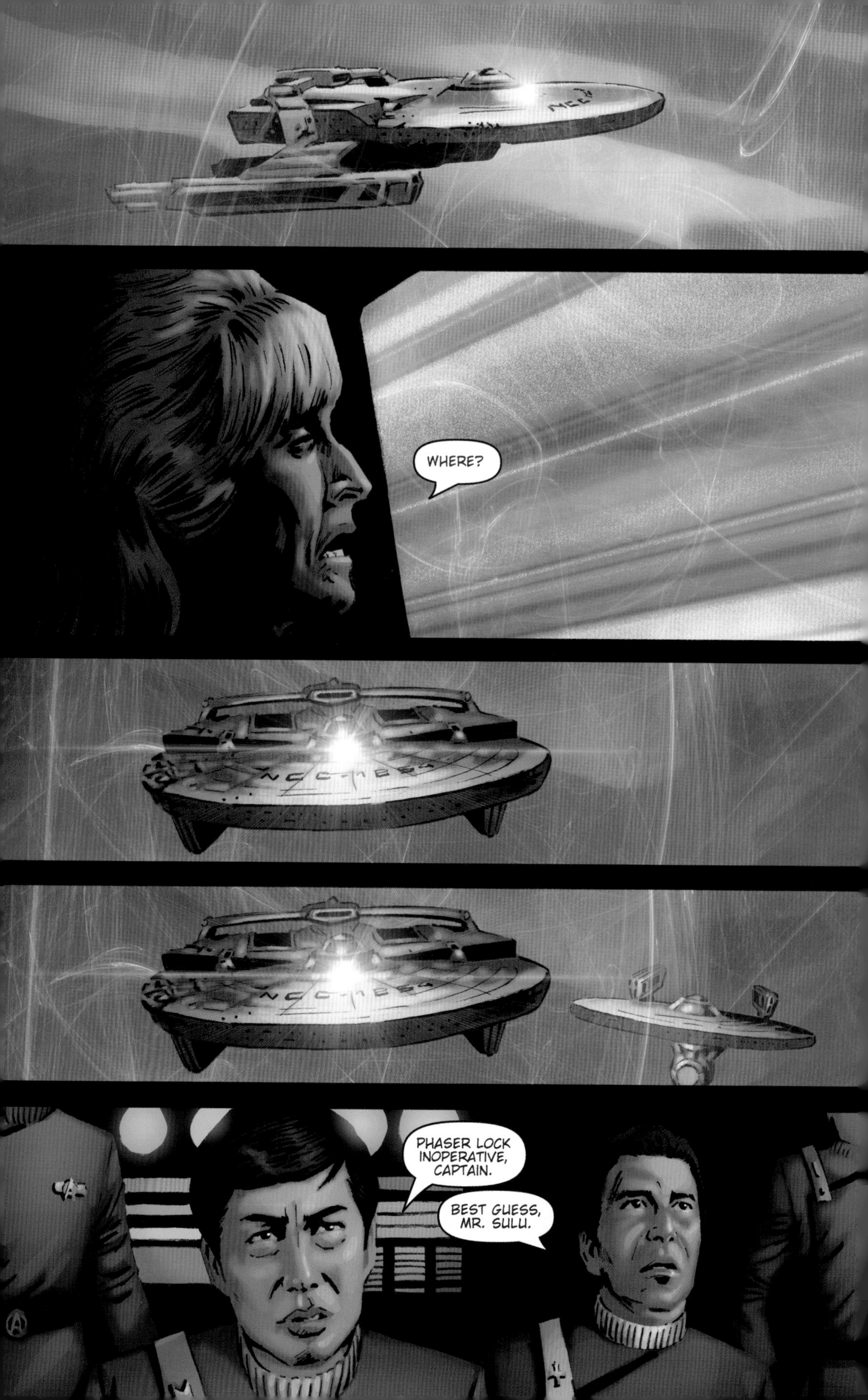
WHERE?
PHASER LOCK INOPERATIVE, CAPTAIN.
BEST GUESS, MR. SULU.

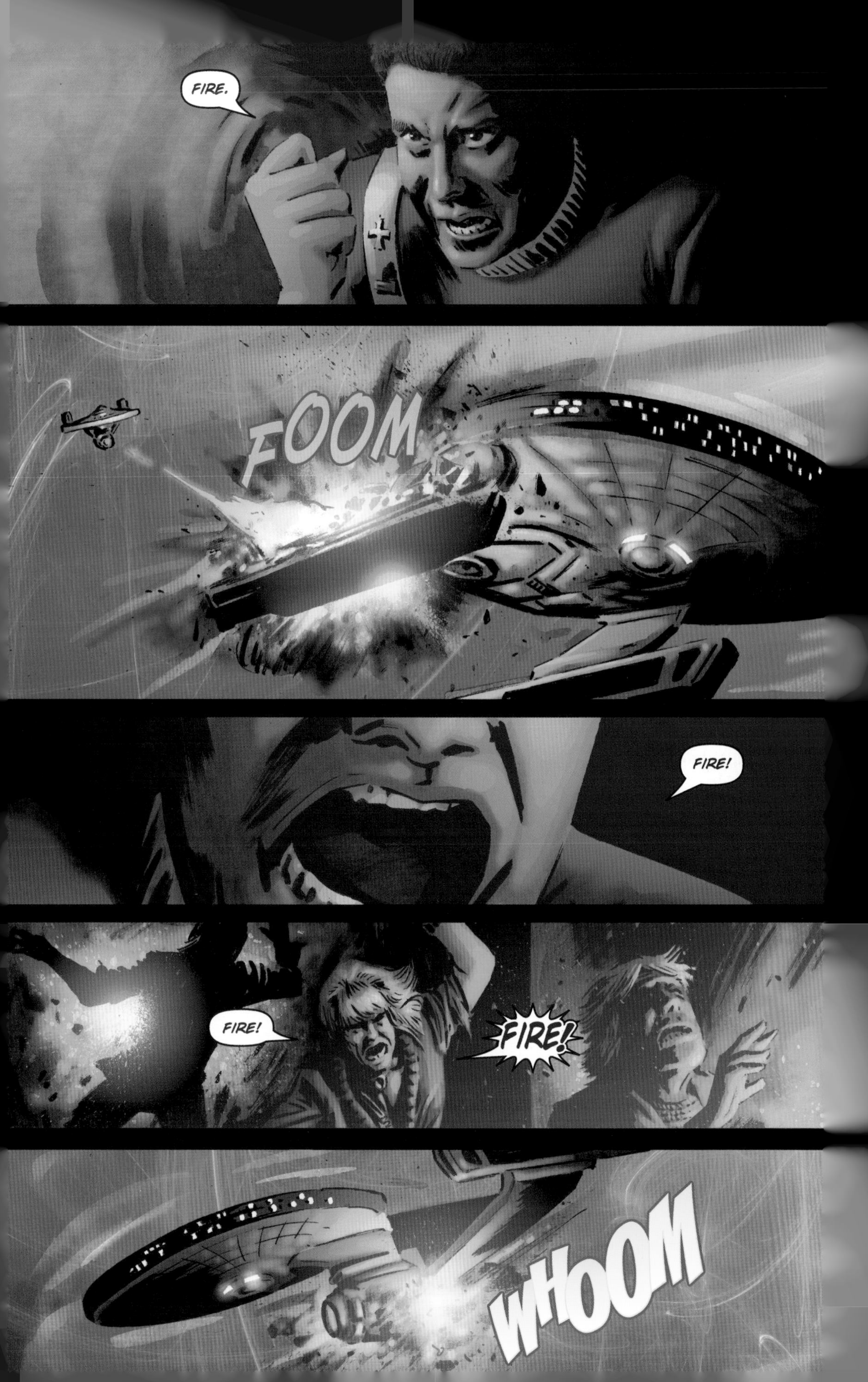
FIRE.
FOOM
FIRE!
FIRE!
FIRE!
WHOOM

BOOM
BOOM

SHA-KOOM

BOOM

SCOTTY. REPORT!

GOT TO TAKE MAINS OFFLINE. THE RADIATION...
...LEAKING...
...UHH...

NO, KIRK.
THE GAME'S NOT OVER.
TO THE LAST, I GRAPPLE WITH THEE...
FROM HELL'S HEART I STAB AT THEE.
FOR HATE'S SAKE, I SPIT MY LAST BREATH...
...AT THEE.
BEEP BBBRRRRRRRMMMMMMM

THERE IS AN ODD ENERGY SIGNATURE COMING FROM THE *RELIANT*.
OH, NO...
IT'S THE GENESIS WAVE. IT'S BUILDING UP TO DETONATION— 4 MINUTES.
WE'LL BEAM ABOARD TO STOP IT.
YOU ***CAN'T***.
SCOTTY, I NEED WARP SPEED IN THREE MINUTES OR WE'RE ALL DEAD!

NO RESPONSE, ADMIRAL.

SULU, GET US OUT OF HERE!

AYE, SIR. I'M DOING EVERYTHING I CAN, BUT WARP IS OFFLINE WHILE WE HAVE THE RADIATION LEAK.

UUH...

ARE YOU OUT OF YOUR VULCAN MIND?
NO HUMAN CAN TOLERATE THE LEVEL OF RADIATION THAT'S IN THERE.
AS YOU ARE FOND OF OBSERVING, DOCTOR, I AM ***NOT*** HUMAN.
YOU'RE NOT GOING IN THERE!

—HUK.

REMEMBER.

FSSSSSSSS

SPOCK!

GET OUT OF THERE!

TIME?
TWO MINUTES AND TEN SECONDS.
ENGINE ROOM! WHAT'S HAPPENING?
SCOTTY!
ANYBODY!
SPOCK, DON'T!
YOU'LL DIE, MAN!
SIR, THE MAINS ARE BACK ON LINE!

TIME.
30 SECONDS, SIR.
WE'RE NOT GOING TO MAKE IT ARE WE?
NO.
MR. SCOTT, *THANK YOU!*
SULU, GO!

ENGINE ROOM, WELL DONE, SCOTTY.

JIM...

BONES?

SPOCK!

STOP!
YOU'LL FLOOD THE WHOLE COMPARTMENT.
HE'LL DIE!

HE'S DEAD ALREADY.

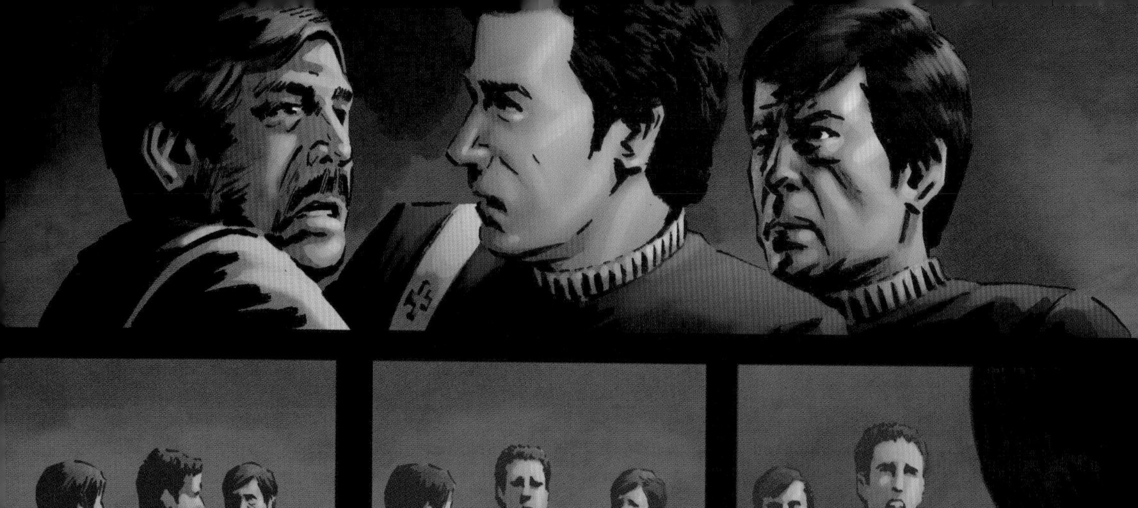

SPOCK.

SHIP...
...OUT OF DANGER?

YES.
DON'T GRIEVE, ADMIRAL.
IT IS LOGICAL.
THE NEEDS OF THE MANY, OUTWEIGH...
...THE NEEDS OF THE FEW...
...OR THE ONE.
KAFF KKAFF
I NEVER TOOK THE KOBAYASHI MARU TEST...
...UNTIL NOW.
WHAT DO YOU THINK... OF MY SOLUTION?
SPOCK...

I HAVE BEEN... AND ALWAYS SHALL BE...
...YOUR FRIEND.
LIVE LONG...
...AND PROSPER.

WE ARE ASSEMBLED HERE TODAY TO PAY FINAL RESPECTS TO OUR HONORED DEAD.
AND YET IT SHOULD BE NOTED THAT IN THE MIDST OF OUR SORROW, THIS DEATH TAKES PLACE IN THE SHADOW OF NEW LIFE...
...THE SUNRISE OF A NEW WORLD— A WORLD THAT OUR BELOVED COMRADE GAVE HIS LIFE TO PROTECT AND NOURISH.
HE DID NOT FEEL THIS SACRIFICE A VAIN OR EMPTY ONE. AND WE WILL NOT DEBATE HIS PROFOUND WISDOM AT THESE PROCEEDINGS.
OF MY FRIEND I CAN ONLY SAY THIS... OF ALL THE SOULS I HAVE ENCOUNTERED IN MY TRAVELS...
...HIS WAS THE MOST...
...HUMAN.

CLAKT
BREEP
COME IN.

I DON'T MEAN TO INTRUDE. CAN WE TALK FOR A MOMENT?
I SHOULD BE ON THE BRIDGE. I POURED MYSELF A DRINK. WOULD YOU LIKE IT?
SAAVIK WAS RIGHT.
YOU NEVER HAVE FACED DEATH.

NO, NOT LIKE THIS.
I HAVEN'T FACED DEATH. I'VE CHEATED DEATH—TRICKED MY WAY OUT OF DEATH.
I KNOW NOTHING.
I WAS WRONG ABOUT YOU AND I'M SORRY.
IS THAT WHAT YOU CAME HERE TO SAY, DAVID?

MAINLY.
AND ALSO...
...THAT I'M PROUD. VERY PROUD...

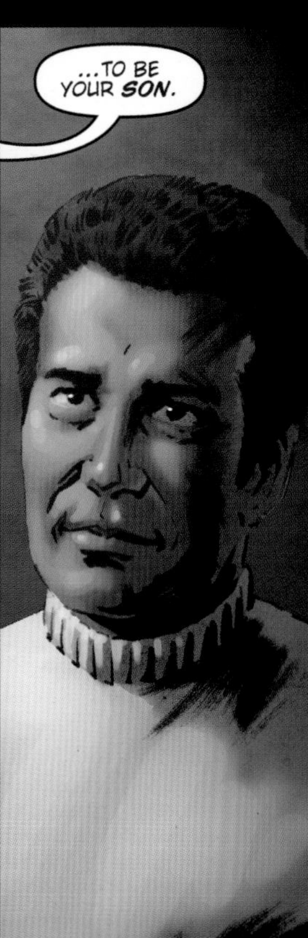
...TO BE YOUR SON.

CAPTAIN'S LOG. STARDATE 8141.6.

STARSHIP *ENTERPRISE* DEPARTING FOR CETI ALPHA V TO PICK UP THE CREW OF THE *U.S.S. RELIANT*.

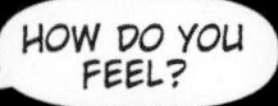

SPACE.

THE FINAL FRONTIER.

THESE ARE THE CONTINUING VOYAGES OF
THE STARSHIP *ENTERPRISE*.

HER ONGOING MISSION,
TO EXPLORE STRANGE NEW WORLDS...

...TO SEEK OUT NEW LIFE FORMS
AND NEW CIVILIZATIONS.

TO BOLDLY GO WHERE
NO MAN HAS GONE...

...BEFORE.

THE END

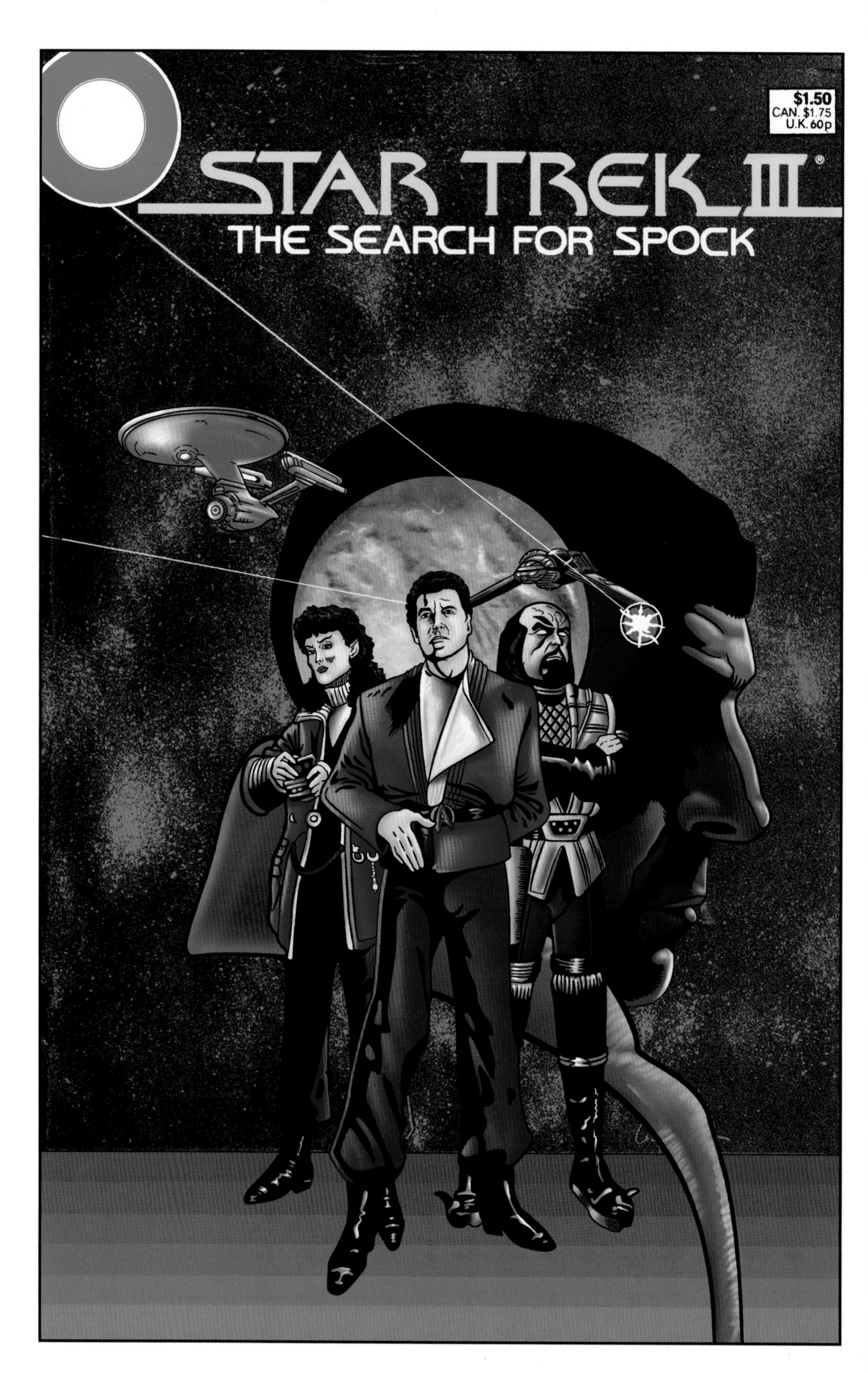
$1.50
CAN. $1.75
U.K. 60p
STAR TREK III
THE SEARCH FOR SPOCK

"SPACE... THE FINAL FRONTIER.

"THESE ARE THE CONTINUING VOYAGES OF THE STARSHIP ENTERPRISE, HER ONGOING MISSION:
"...TO EXPLORE STRANGE NEW WORLDS...

"...TO SEEK OUT NEW LIFE-FORMS AND NEW CIVILIZATIONS...
"...TO BOLDLY GO WHERE NO MAN HAS GONE...

"...BEFORE!"
MARK IV
PARAMOUNT PICTURES PRESENTS:

STAR TREK III
THE SEARCH FOR SPOCK

BASED ON A SCREENPLAY BY **HARVE BENNETT**

ADAPTED BY: MIKE W. BARR, WRITER · TOM SUTTON and RICARDO VILLAGRÁN, ARTISTS · JOHN COSTANZA, LETTERER · MICHELE WOLFMAN, COLORIST · MARV WOLFMAN, EDITOR

THE GENESIS PLANET; STARDATE: 8210.3
WE ARE APPROACHING DESTINATION PLANET AT POINT ZERO THREE FIVE...
...SO NOTED IN SHIP'S LOG, SIR.
VERY WELL, LIEUTENANT. EXECUTE STANDARD ORBITAL APPROACH.
STANDARD ORBIT, AYE.
COMMUNICATIONS, SEND A CODED MESSAGE TO STARFLEET COMMAND, PRIORITY ONE...
"...FEDERATION SCIENCE VESSEL GRISSOM ARRIVING GENESIS PLANET, MUTARA SECTOR, TO BEGIN RESEARCH.
"AS ORDERED, FULL SECURITY PROCEDURES ARE IN EFFECT. J.T. ESTEBAN, COMMANDING."
AYE, SIR, CODING NOW.
DR. MARCUS, IT'S YOUR PLANET.
THANK YOU, CAPTAIN ESTEBAN. BEGIN SCANNING, PLEASE.
THIS IS WHERE THE FUN BEGINS, SAAVIK!
JUST LIKE YOUR FATHER... SO HUMAN.
SCANNING SECTOR ONE: FOLIAGE IS AT FULLY DEVELOPED STATE OF GROWTH. TEMPERATURE, 22.2 DEGREES CELSIUS.

NCC
SECTOR 2... READING DESERT TERRAIN. MINIMAL VEGETATION, TEMPERATURE 39.4°.
SECTOR 3: SUB-TROPICAL VEGETATION, TEMPERATURE --TEMPERATURE DECREASING RAPIDLY...?

IT'S *SNOW!* SNOW IN THE SAME SECTOR! FANTASTIC!
FASCINATING.
ALL VARIETIES OF LAND AND WEATHER KNOWN TO EARTH WITHIN A FEW HOURS' WALK!

YOU MUST BE VERY PROUD OF WHAT YOU AND YOUR MOTHER HAVE CREATED
WELL, IT'S A LITTLE *EARLY* TO CELEBRATE...
BEEP BEEP BEEP

I'M READING A METALLIC MASS IN THE SAME SECTOR.
IT'S ON SURFACE... A *MANUFACTURED* OBJECT.
ONLY ONE THING IT COULD BE... TRY A SHORT-RANGE SCAN.

APPROXIMATELY TWO METERS LONG... CYLINDRICAL IN FORM...
A *PHOTON TUBE!*
COULD IT BE *SPOCK'S?*

IT HAS TO BE! GRAVITATIONAL FIELDS WERE IN FLUX... IT MUST HAVE SOFT LANDED!
COMMUNICATIONS, IN CODE TO STARFLEET: *"CAPTAIN SPOCK'S TUBE LOCATED INTACT ON GENESIS SURFACE...*
"WILL RELAY MORE DATA ON SUBSEQUENT ORBITS."

CODING YOUR MESSAGE, SIR.

"CAPTAIN'S LOG, PERSONAL: WITH MOST OF OUR BATTLE DAMAGE REPAIRED, WE ARE ALMOST HOME, AND YET I FEEL... AND I WONDER WHY.
"PERHAPS IT IS THE ERRATIC BEHAVIOR OF DR. McCOY...OR THE EMPTINESS OF THIS VESSEL: MOST OF OUR TRAINEE CREW HAS BEEN REASSIGNED...
NCC1701
"...LIEUTENANT SAAVIK AND MY SON DAVID ARE EXPLORING A NEW WORLD...
"...AND THE ENTERPRISE FEELS LIKE A HOUSE WITH ALL ITS CHILDREN GONE.
"NO...MORE EMPTY EVEN THAN THAT.
"THE NEWS OF SPOCK'S TUBE HAS SHAKEN ME...
"...IT SEEMS THAT I HAVE LEFT THE NOBLEST PART OF MYSELF BACK THERE...ON THAT NEWBORN PLANET."
STATUS, MR. SULU?
ON COURSE, ADMIRAL. ESTIMATING ARRIVAL AT SPACEDOCK IN 2.1 HOURS.

VERY WELL. MR. CHEKOV, TAKE THE SCIENCE STATION, PLEASE, FOR PRE-APPROACH SCAN.
...
YES, SIR.
UHURA, ANY RESPONSE FROM STARFLEET ON OUR PROJECT GENESIS INQUIRIES?
NO, SIR, NO RESPONSE.
ODD. SCOTTY, PROGRESS REPORT?

ALMOST DONE, SIR. YOU'LL BE FULLY AUTOMATED BY THE TIME WE DOCK.
EXCELLENT TIMING, MR SCOTT; YOU'VE FIXED THE BARN DOOR AFTER THE HORSE HAS COME HOME.
HOW MUCH REFIT TIME TILL WE CAN TAKE HER OUT AGAIN?
8 WEEKS, SIR... BUT YOU DON'T HAVE 8 WEEKS, SO I'LL DO IT FOR YE IN 2!
MR. SCOTT, HAVE YOU ALWAYS MULTIPLIED YOUR REPAIR BY A FACTOR OF 4?
CERTAINLY, SIR. HOW ELSE CAN I KEEP MUH REPUTATION AS A MIRACLE WORKER?
YOUR REPUTATION IS SECURE, SCOTTY.

MR. SULU, TAKE THE CONN. I'LL BE IN MY QUARTERS.
AYE, SIR.
SIR...?

...I WAS WONDERING... ARE THEY PLANNING A CEREMONY WHEN WE GET IN...? I MEAN, A RECEPTION...?
A HERO'S WELCOME, SON? IS THAT WHAT YOU'D LIKE? WELL, GOD KNOWS THERE SHOULD BE...

...THIS TIME WE PAID FOR THE PARTY WITH OUR DEAREST BLOOD.

CAPTAIN'S QUARTERS.

BING
HELLO, BONES.
JIM.

ARE YOU PLANNING TO SHAVE TODAY?
QUO VADIS, ADMIRAL...?
WHAT IS THAT SUPPOSED TO MEAN?
"WHERE ARE YOU GOING?" WHAT IS OUR DESTINATION?

WE'LL BE ORBITING EARTH IN 2 HOURS.
THEN WE'RE HEADING IN THE WRONG DIRECTION.
BONES, DON'T DO THIS. THIS IS ME, JIM...YOUR FRIEND.

AND I HAVE BEEN, AND ALWAYS SHALL BE, YOURS.
DAMN IT, BONES, DON'T QUOTE SPOCK TO ME! I HAVE ENOUGH PAIN OF MY OWN AND I DON'T NEED YOUR-- SELF-INDULGENCE!

YOU LEFT ME. YOU LEFT ME ON GENESIS.
WHY DID YOU DO THAT?
WHAT THE *HELL* ARE YOU SAYING?

I DON'T KNOW, I JUST...
WHY DID WE LEAVE SPOCK?
BONES! YOU MUST DEAL WITH THE *TRUTH!*
HE'S GONE.

SPOCK IS *GONE*. AND WE *BOTH* HAVE TO LIVE WITH THAT.
I CAN'T GET HIM OUT OF MY HEAD, JIM. AND I'D GIVE THE WHOLE STATE OF GEORGIA IF SOMEONE COULD TELL ME *WHY*.

SOMEWHERE IN ORGANIAN SPACE...
STEADY, BOYS... KEEP SCANNING...

I THOUGHT YOU PEOPLE WERE *RELIABLE*... WHERE THE HELL IS HE?
HE HAS BEEN HERE FOR SOME TIME. I CAN FEEL HIS PRESENCE.
DON'T GIVE ME YOUR KLINGON MUMBO-JUMBO-- THERE AIN'T ANOTHER VESSEL IN THIS WHOLE DAMN *QUADRANT!*

PUT ME ON THE HAILING FREQUENCY.
SURE--WHATEVER GAMES YOU WANNA PLAY.
COMMANDER KRUGE, THIS IS VALKRIS. I HAVE OBTAINED THE FEDERATION DATA, AND AM READY TO TRANS-MIT.

WELL DONE, VALKRIS... STAND BY.
DISENSAGE CLOAKING DEVICE!
WHAT THE HELL...?
TRANSMIT DATA!
TRANSMISSION COMPLETED. YOU WILL FIND IT ESSENTIAL TO YOUR MISSION.
THEN YOU HAVE SEEN IT?
I HAVE, MY LORD.
THAT IS UNFORTUNATE.
I UNDERSTAND.
HELMSMAN, THRUSTERS!
WHAT'S GOING ON? WHEN DO WE GET PAID OFF...?
SOON, CAPTAIN... QUITE SOON.
SUCCESS, MY LORD-- AND MY LOVE.
YOU WILL BE REMEMBERED WITH HONOR.
FIRE.
WROOOM

I'LL BE IN MY QUARTERS. EXECUTE COURSE TO THE FEDERATION BOUNDARY... AND FEED HIM!
GRRRRRR
YES, MY LORD!
NEW ORBIT COMMENCING... COMING UP ON SECTOR 3...
SHORT-RANGE SCAN.
I DON'T BELIEVE IT!
WHAT IS IT?
IF EQUIPMENT IS FUNCTIONING PROPERLY, INDICATIONS ARE--
--AN ANIMAL LIFE-FORM.
YOU SAID THERE WOULDN'T BE ANY.
THERE SHOULDN'T BE ANY! ONLY PLANT FORMS WERE BUILT INTO THE GENESIS MATRIX.
VERIFIED; AN UNIDENTIFIABLE LIFE-FORM READING.
WHY DON'T WE BEAM IT UP?
OH, NO, YOU DON'T! CAN YOU GUARANTEE THERE'S NO DANGER OF CONTAMINATION?
CAPTAIN...
NOT FROM HERE, NO.
...BEAMING DOWN TO THE PLANET'S SURFACE IS PERMITTED...
"...IF THE CAPTAIN DECIDES THE MISSION IS VITAL AND REASONABLY FREE OF DANGER." I KNOW THE BOOK TOO, SAAVIK.
CAPTAIN, PLEASE-- WE'VE GOT TO FIND OUT WHAT IT IS...
...OR WHO.
ALL RIGHT-- GET YOUR GEAR.

SPACEDOCK CONTROL, THIS IS ENTERPRISE; READY FOR DOCKING MANEUVER.
AFFIRMATIVE, ENTERPRISE. ENJOY THE RIDE, AND WELCOME HOME.
WOULD YOU LOOK AT THAT?!
MY FRIENDS, THE GREAT EXPERIMENT-- EXCELSIOR, READY FOR HER TRIAL RUN...

SHE'S SUPPOSED TO HAVE TRANSWARP DRIVE...
AYE, AND IF MY GRANDMOTHER HAD WHEELS, SHE'D BE A WAGON.

MR. SCOTT--
I'M SORRY, SIR, BUT THERE'S NOTHIN' NEEDED FOR SPACE TRAVEL THAT THIS OLD GIRL DOESN'T ALREADY HAVE!

COME, COME, SCOTTY. YOUNG MINDS, FRESH IDEAS.
BE TOLERANT.
ADMIRAL..

...I AM READING A LIFE-FORM ON "C" DECK...IN MR. SPOCK'S QUARTERS.
MR. CHEKOV, THIS ENTIRE CREW SEEMS ON THE EDGE OF OBSESSIVE BEHAVIOR CONCERNING MR. SPOCK!
I ORDERED HIS QUARTERS SEALED!

YES, SIR, I SEALED THE ROOM MYSELF! NEVERTHELESS--
ALL RIGHT, I'LL HAVE A LOOK.

JIM...
SPOCK...?
WHO'S THERE?

WHO?

BONES? BONES, WHAT THE HELL ARE YOU DOING?
CLIMB THE STEPS, JIM... THE STEPS OF MOUNT SELEYA...
BONES, MOUNT SELEYA IS ON VULCAN! WE'RE --

REMEMBER!
REMEMBER!

ADMIRAL, STARFLEET COMMANDER MORROW IS ON HIS WAY FOR INSPECTION.
UHURA, GET THE MEDICS DOWN HERE! GET THEM NOW!

BONES, IT'S ALL RIGHT...
...IT'S ALL RIGHT...

TEN-SHUN!
WELCOME ABOARD, ADMIRAL.
WELCOME HOME, JIM.

WELL DONE. YOU'LL BE RECEIVING STARFLEET'S HIGHEST COMMENDATIONS, AND--MORE IMPORTANTLY, I'M SURE--EXTENDED SHORE LEAVE.

ALL BUT YOU, MR. SCOTT; THEY NEED YOUR WISDOM ON THE EXCELSIOR. REPORT THERE TOMORROW AS CAPTAIN OF ENGINEERING.
BUT, SIR--THE ENTERPRISE REFIT WILL NEED A PRACTICED HAND... IT COULD TAKE MONTHS.

MR. SCOTT, THERE WON'T BE A REFIT! THE ENTERPRISE IS 20 YEARS OLD; WE THINK HER DAY IS OVER.
BUT... WE WERE HOPING TO TAKE HER BACK TO GENESIS...!

OUT OF THE QUESTION, JIM! UNTIL THE FEDERATION COUNCIL MAKES POLICY, CONSIDER GENESIS A QUARANTINED PLANET--
--AND A FORBIDDEN SUBJECT!

"...IT WAS THIS PREMATURE DETONATION OF THE GENESIS DEVICE...

"...THAT RESULTED IN THE CREATION OF THE GENESIS PLANET--"
I HAVE SEEN ENOUGH!

SPEAK!
GREAT POWER...TO CONTROL...DOMINATE... DESTROY. IF IT WORKS!
IMPRESSIVE... POSSIBILITIES ARE ENDLESS...COLONIES, RESOURCES...
WE ARE GOING TO THIS "PLANET," MALTZ. WE WILL ACT FOR THE PRESERVATION OF OUR RACE! WITH ITS SECRET, WE WILL DOMINATE...DESTROY!
STATION, WEAKLING!
Y-YES, MY LORD!

APPROACHING NEUTRAL ZONE, MY LORD!
ENGAGE CLOAKING DEVICE!

...DO YOU CONCUR?
AFFIRMATIVE, CAPTAIN. OUR READINGS ARE WELL BELOW DANGER LEVEL. HOWEVER, THEY ALSO INDICATE GEOLOGIC INSTABILITY.
WE'RE NOT HERE TO INVESTIGATE GEOLOGIC AGING, SAAVIK! COME ON!
WHATEVER IT IS, IT'S OVER THERE.
SPOCK'S TUBE? BUT THAT--
DAVID, AT ITS BASE.
GRISSOM TO LANDING PARTY; WE HAVE YOU APPROACHING RADIOACTIVE INDICATIONS...
THERE'S YOUR "LIFE-FORM," SAAVIK. THESE WERE MICROBES ON THE TUBE'S SURFACE... THEY WERE FRUITFUL, AND MULTIPLIED.
MARK IV
BUT HOW COULD THEY HAVE EVOLVED SO QUICKLY..?
I'M STILL GETTING A RADIOACTIVE READING, SAAVIK-- FROM THE TUBE.
MARK IV

ARK IV

SAAVIK...
MARK IV

...HE'S GONE.

WHAT'S THIS?
SPOCK'S BURIAL ROBE.

OOOWWWWOOOO

TO ABSENT FRIENDS.
ADMIRAL, WHAT'S GOING TO HAPPEN TO THE ENTERPRISE?

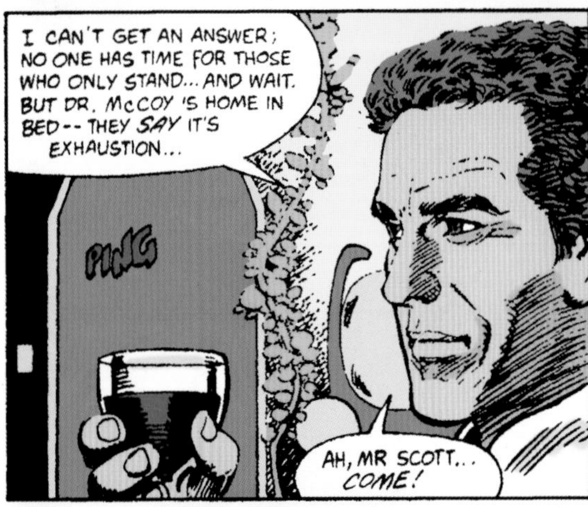
I CAN'T GET AN ANSWER; NO ONE HAS TIME FOR THOSE WHO ONLY STAND... AND WAIT. BUT DR. McCOY 'S HOME IN BED -- THEY SAY IT'S EXHAUSTION...
PING
AH, MR SCOTT... COME!

WHO--?

SAREK!
I WILL SPEAK WITH YOU ALONE, KIRK.

SAREK, I WOULD HAVE RETURNED TO VULCAN. TO TELL YOU HOW BRAVELY YOUR SON DIED..
YOU MISS THE POINT, KIRK. THEN AND NOW ONLY SPOCK'S BODY "DIED"! YOU SHOULD HAVE COME WITH IT TO VULCAN, AS HE REQUESTED.

YOU MUST BELIEVE ME WHEN I TELL YOU THAT SPOCK MADE NO REQUEST OF ME!
...
KIRK, MAY I JOIN YOUR MIND? I MUST HAVE YOUR THOUGHTS.

"...HE SPOKE OF YOUR FRIENDSHIP, KIRK."
"YES..."
"...SPOCK ASKED YOU NOT TO GRIEVE..."
"...YES..."
"...THE NEEDS OF THE MANY OUTWEIGH..."
"...THE NEEDS OF THE FEW..."
"...OR THE ONE..."
"...SPOCK, MY FRIEND..."
"I HAVE BEEN... AND ALWAYS SHALL BE...YOUR FRIEND. LIVE LONG... AND PROSPER!"
"NO!"

NO!

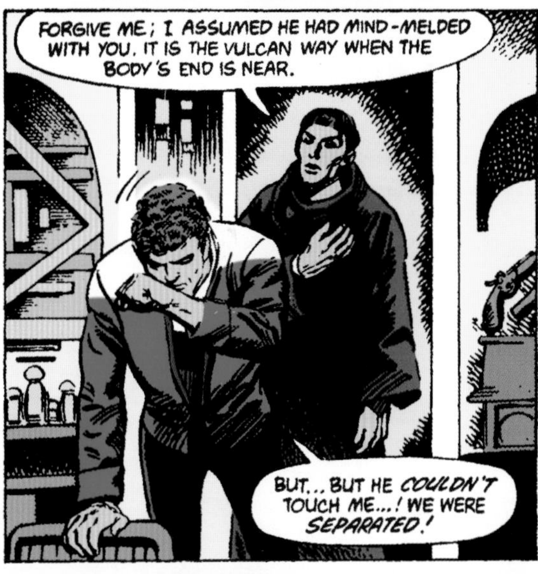
FORGIVE ME; I ASSUMED HE HAD MIND-MELDED WITH YOU. IT IS THE VULCAN WAY WHEN THE BODY'S END IS NEAR.
BUT... BUT HE COULDN'T TOUCH ME...! WE WERE SEPARATED!

I SEE. THEN HIS KATRA, HIS LIVING SPIRIT... EVERYTHING THAT HE WAS, EVERYTHING THAT HE KNEW..., IS LOST.
WAIT, SAREK!... WHAT IF HE MELDED WITH SOMEONE ELSE?!

...DOCTOR, I HAVE NO TIME TO DISCUSS THIS LOGICALLY--REMEMBER.
THERE! HE MELDED WITH BONES! MY GOD, BONES...!

ONE ALIVE, ONE NOT. YET BOTH IN PAIN. YOU MUST BRING THEM TO MOUNT SELEYA ON VULCAN. ONLY THERE CAN BOTH FIND PEACE.
WHAT YOU ASK IS DIFFICULT...

YOU WILL FIND A WAY, KIRK. IF YOU HONOR THEM BOTH, YOU MUST.
I WILL.
I SWEAR.

OOOWMMMOOOO
THAT CRY...! WE HEAR IT WHENEVER THE GROUND QUAKES! WHAT IS IT?
DAVID, LOOK.

NO, ABSOLUTELY *NOT*, JIM! IT'S OUT OF THE *QUESTION!* THE RULES ARE --
DON'T QUOTE *RULES* TO ME, HARRY! WE'RE TALKING ABOUT *LOYALTY*...
... AND *SACRIFICE!* SPOCK *DIED* FOR US, McCOY IS SUFFERING DEEP EMOTIONAL DAMAGE--

THIS BUSINESS ABOUT SPOCK AND McCOY... JIM, I HAVE NEVER UNDERSTOOD VULCAN MYSTICISM, BUT--
HARRY, YOU DON'T *HAVE* TO BELIEVE! I'M NOT EVEN SURE *I* BELIEVE! BUT IF SPOCK *HAS* AN ETERNAL SOUL, THEN IT'S *MY* RESPONSIBILITY!

HARRY, GIVE ME BACK THE *ENTERPRISE!* WITH--
NO!

THE COUNCIL HAS ORDERED THAT NO SHIP BUT THE *GRISSOM* IS TO GO TO GENESIS!
JIM, KEEP THIS UP AND YOU'LL *DESTROY* YOURSELF! DO YOU HEAR ME?
YES... I HEAR YOU... I JUST HAD TO *TRY.*

THE WORD, SIR?
STARFLEET HEADQUARTERS
THE WORD IS *NO.*

I AM THEREFORE GOING ANYWAY.

COUNT ON OUR HELP, SIR.
I'LL NEED IT, SULU.
SHALL I ALERT DR. McCOY?
YES...

"...HE HAS A LONG JOURNEY AHEAD."
BAR
ALTAIR WATER.
NOT YOUR USUAL POISON, DOC.

TO EXPECT ONE TO ORDER POISON IN A BAR IS NOT *LOGICAL*.
EXCUSE ME... I'M ON MEDICATION.
GOT IT.
HELLO. YOU ARE BEING McCOY, FROM *ENTERPRISE*?

YOU SEEK I. AVAILABLE SHIP STANDS BY.
GOOD. HOW SOON AND HOW MUCH?
HOW SOON IS NOW. HOW MUCH IS WHERE.

WHERE?... SOMEWHERE IN THE MUTARA SECTOR.
YOU NAME PLACE, YES?

ALL RIGHT, DAMMIT, IT'S GENESIS!
GENESIS?!
I'M SORRY, DOCTOR...

...BUT YOU DON'T WANT TO BE DISCUSSING THIS IN PUBLIC.
AND WHO THE HELL ARE YOU?

FEDERATION SECURITY, SIR.
WHAT IN--?

KRASSSSH

LET ME GO!

?

BAR
YOU'RE GOING TO GET A NICE LONG *REST*, DOCTOR.

THIS WAY...
BEEP BEEP BEEP

THERE.

THE GENESIS WAVE...

...HIS CELLS COULD HAVE BEEN REGENERATED... REFORMED...!
SAAVIK TO GRISSOM. THE LIFE-FORM READING IS CAUSED BY A VULCAN CHILD, EIGHT TO TEN EARTH YEARS IN AGE.
HOW DID HE GET THERE?

IT IS DR. MARCUS' OPINION THAT THIS IS--
--THAT THE GENESIS EFFECT HAS IN SOME WAY REGENERATED...
...CAPTAIN SPOCK.

REQUEST PERMISSION TO BEAM ABOARD IMMEDIATELY.
FIRST I'M GOING TO CONTACT STARFLEET AND GET INSTRUCTIONS.

SIR, I'M SURE STARFLEET WOULD--
...AND BE ADVISED WE ARE READING A SEVERE AND UNNATURAL AGE CURVE ON THE PLANET. BE CAREFUL.

SOMETHING'S JAMMING OUR TRANSMISSION, SIR... AN ENERGY SURGE FROM ASTERN.
ON SCREEN.

OH, MY GOD!
RED ALERT! RAISE--

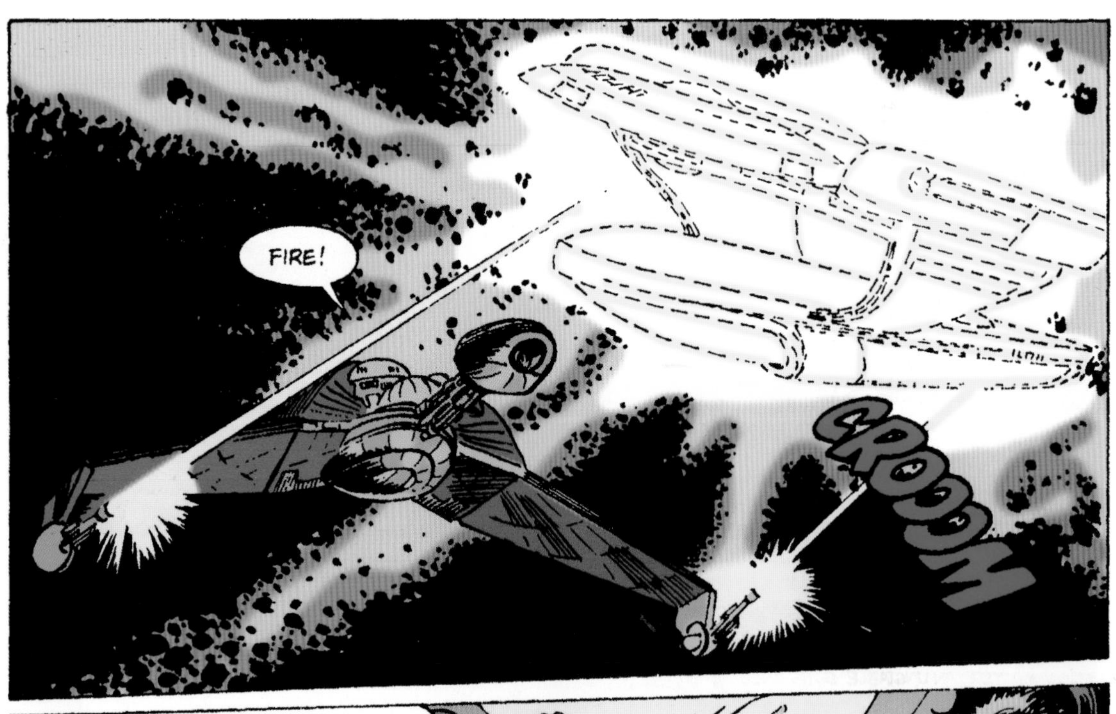
FIRE!
CROOOM

I TOLD YOU, DISABLE THEIR ENGINE SECTION ONLY! I WANTED PRISONERS!
GRRRRR
A FORTUNATE MISTAKE, SIR...
ANIMAL!
SIR, MAY I SUGGEST--

SAY THE WRONG THING, TORG, AND I WILL KILL YOU TOO!
THERE ARE LIFE-SIGNS ON THE PLANET, MY LORD. PERHAPS THE VERY SCIENTISTS-- THE PRISONERS--YOU SEEK.

VERY GOOD. PREPARE A LANDING FORCE.

GRISSOM... THIS IS SAAVIK... COME IN, PLEASE...
NO ANSWER.
WHAT HAPPENED TO THEM?

LOGIC INDICATES THE GRISSOM HAS BEEN DESTROYED-- PERHAPS BY AN ENEMY ATTACK.
HOW CAN YOU BE *LOGICAL* AT A TIME LIKE THIS? WE HAVE TO GET THE HELL *OFF* THIS PLANET!

THIS PLANET IS NOT WHAT YOU INTENDED, OR HOPED FOR, IS IT?
NOT EXACTLY...
WHY?

I USED *PROTOMATTER* IN THE GENESIS MATRIX.
PROTOMATTER; AN UNSTABLE SUBSTANCE WHICH EVERY ETHICAL SCIENTIST IN THE GALAXY HAS DENOUNCED AS DANGEROUSLY UNPREDICTABLE.

IT WAS THE ONLY WAY TO SOLVE CERTAIN PROBLEMS... BUT MY MOTHER KNEW *NOTHING* ABOUT IT!

IF I HADN'T, IT MIGHT HAVE BEEN YEARS BEFORE--
AND HOW MANY HAVE PAID THE PRICE FOR YOUR IMPATIENCE? HOW MANY HAVE DIED?... HOW MANY MAY *YET* DIE?

YOU GOT *TWO MINUTES*, ADMIRAL...

...BEFORE THEY MOVE YOUR FRIEND TO THE FEDERATION FUNNY FARM.
I SEE...

...THEN I'LL TRY NOT TO OVERSTAY MY *WELCOME*.
JIM?

THAT'S *NOT* VERY DAMN FUNNY!
SHHH. HOW MANY FINGERS?
JIM, WHAT'S *WRONG* WITH ME?

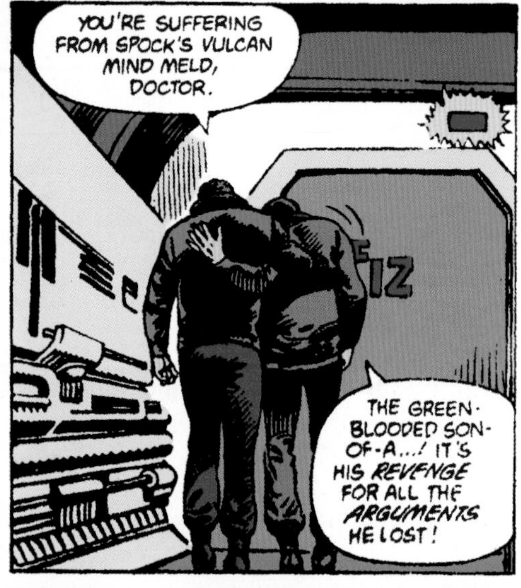
YOU'RE SUFFERING FROM SPOCK'S VULCAN MIND MELD, DOCTOR.
FIZ
THE GREEN-BLOODED SON-OF-A...! IT'S HIS *REVENGE* FOR ALL THE *ARGUMENTS* HE LOST!

WHAT THE HELL'S GOING--

HIIYAAAA

I TOLD HIM NOT TO CALL ME "TINY"...
THE SIDE ELEVATOR... QUICKLY!

UNIT TWO; THIS IS ONE. THE KOBAYASHI MARU HAS SET SAIL FOR THE PROMISED LAND. ACKNOWLEDGE.
MESSAGE ACKNOWLEDGED. ALL UNITS VILL BE INFORMED.

YOU'RE TAKIN' ME TO THE "PROMISED LAND"?
WHAT ARE FRIENDS FOR?
AH, MR. SCOTT. CALLING IT A NIGHT?
ER...YES, CAPTAIN STYLES.
USS EXCELSIOR

TURNING IN MYSELF. LOOKING FORWARD TO BREAKING SOME OF THE ENTERPRISE'S SPEED RECORDS TOMORROW.
WELL, IF ANY SHIP CAN DO IT, SIR...
INDEED. AND I'M CERTAIN YOUR CONTRIBUTION WILL NOT BE FORGOTTEN, MR. SCOTT.
OH, I'M SURE A' THAT, SIR. GOOD NIGHT.
SUTTON
VILLACRAN

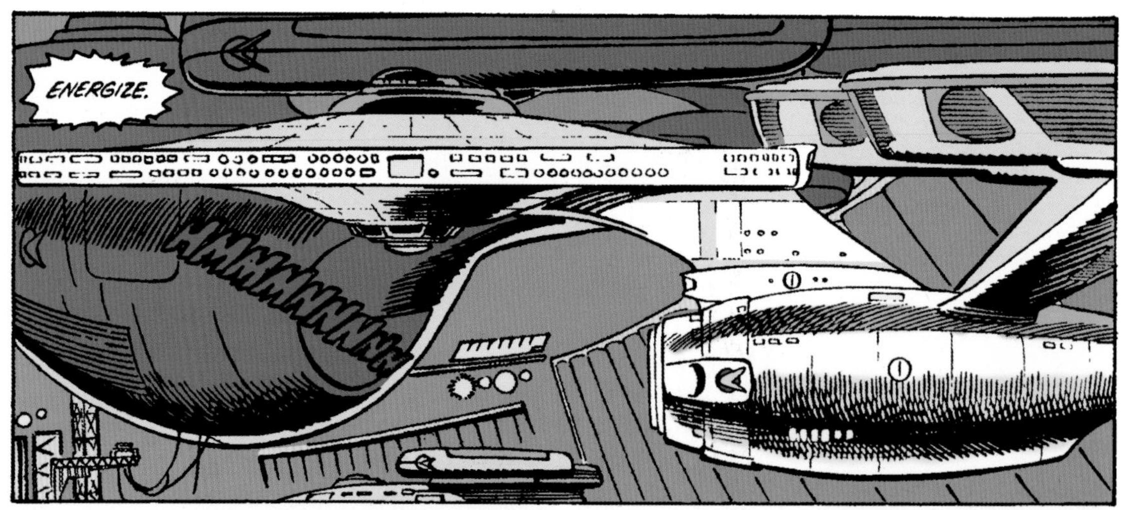
ENERGIZE.
HMMMMNNNNN

VELCOME HOME, MR. SCOTT.
THANK YOU, CHEKOV... LET'S GET SOME LIFE IN THE OLD GIRL.

I SAID, BACK IN THAT CLOSET, MISTER, BEFORE I PHASER YOUR TAIL TO THE WALL!
OKAY, OKAY!
OLD CITY TRANSPORTER STATION
SLAM
RESTRICTED AREA

THANK YOU, UHURA. WILL YOU BE ABLE TO HANDLE YOUR... COLLEAGUE?
I'LL HAVE HIM EATING OUT OF MY HAND, ADMIRAL. YOU'D BETTER GET GOING NOW.

SEE YOU ALL AT THE RENDEZVOUS. ALL HOPES.
HMMMMNNNN

AS PROMISED, SHE'S ALL YOURS, ADMIRAL...

...ALL SYSTEMS AUTOMATED AND READY. A CHIMPANZEE AND TWO TRAINEES COULD RUN 'ER.
THANK YOU, MR. SCOTT. I'LL TRY NOT TO TAKE THAT PERSONALLY.

MY FRIENDS... I CAN'T ASK YOU TO GO ANY FURTHER. DR. McCOY AND I *HAVE* TO DO THIS...
...THE REST OF YOU DO NOT.

ADMIRAL, VE ARE LOSING PRECIOUS TIME.
WHAT COURSE, PLEASE, ADMIRAL?
I'D BE GRATEFUL, ADMIRAL, IF YOU'D GIVE THE WORD.

GENTLEMEN... MAY THE WIND BE AT OUR BACKS.
STATIONS, PLEASE!

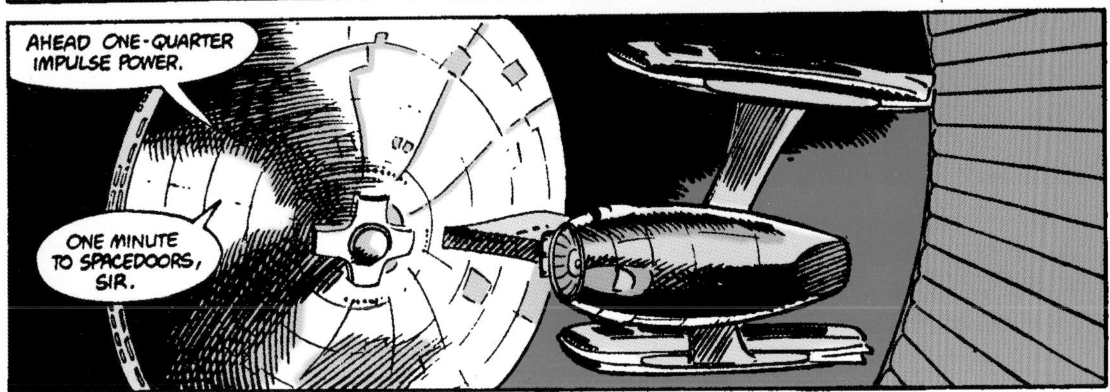
AHEAD ONE-QUARTER IMPULSE POWER.
ONE MINUTE TO SPACEDOORS, SIR.

THE SPACEDOORS--YOU'RE JUST GONNA... WALK THROUGH THEM?
CALM YOURSELF, BONES.
SIR, THE EXCELSIOR IS POWERING UP WITH ORDERS TO PURSUE, UNLESS WE SURRENDER THIS VESSEL! SHOULD I--?
NO REPLY, CHEKOV. SCREEN ON.
MY GOD, SHE'S GAINING ON US JUST SITTING THERE!
STATUS?
ALL AUTOMATES READY AND FUNCTIONING. ALL SPEEDS AVAILABLE THROUGH TRANSWARP DRIVE, SIR!
INCREDIBLE MACHINE! HELMSMAN, ONE-QUARTER IMPULSE POWER.
THIRTY SECONDS TO SPACE-DOORS, SIR.
ALL RIGHT, SCOTTY, OPEN THE DOORS.
...MISTER SCOTT, OPEN THE DOORS...!
YES, SIR, WORKIN' ON IT...
...THERE!
WE HAVE...WE HAVE CLEARED SPACEDOORS, SIR.
BRING HER AROUND, MR. SULU--FULL IMPULSE POWER!

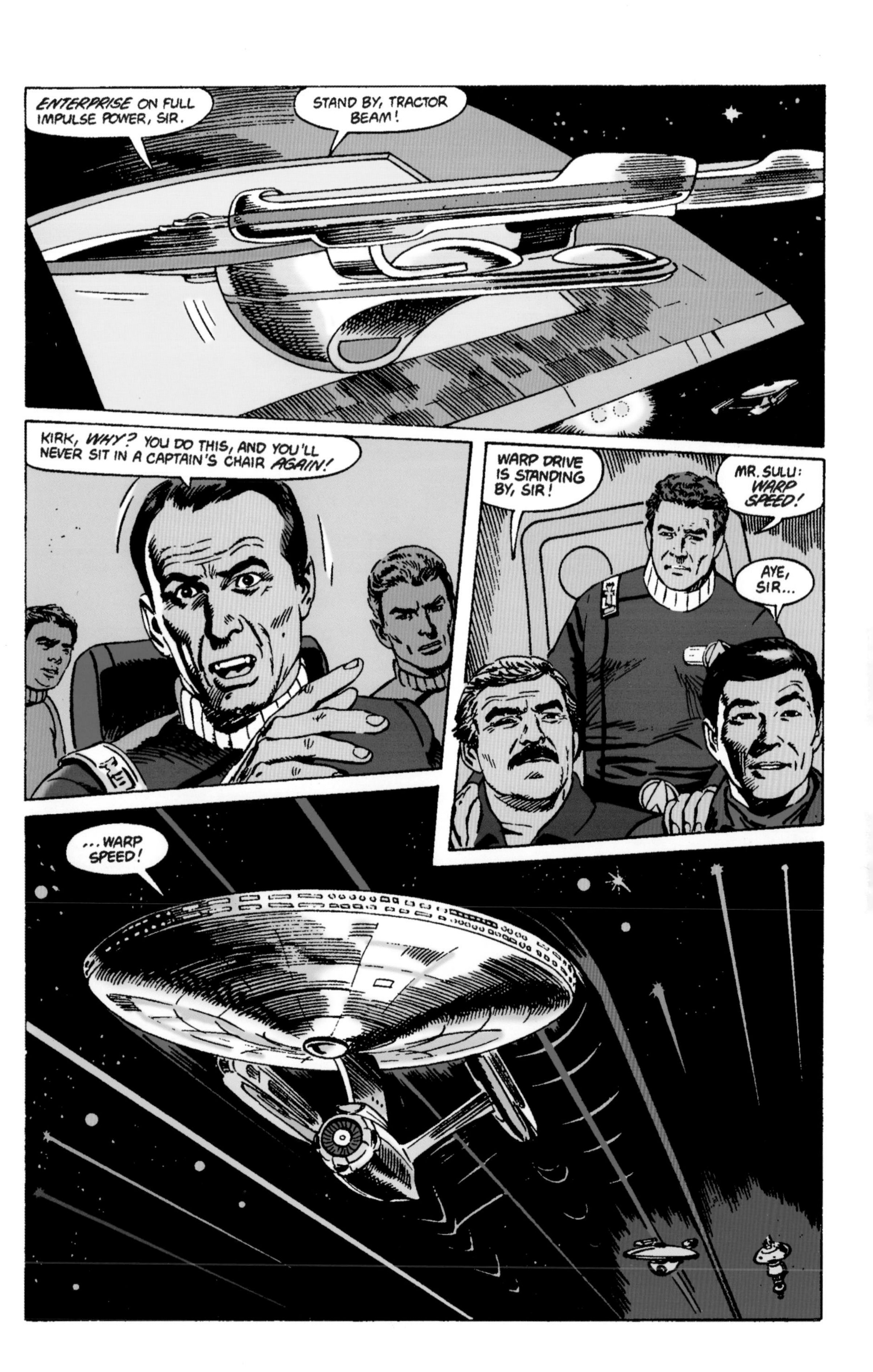
ENTERPRISE ON FULL IMPULSE POWER, SIR.
STAND BY, TRACTOR BEAM!
KIRK, WHY? YOU DO THIS, AND YOU'LL NEVER SIT IN A CAPTAIN'S CHAIR AGAIN!
WARP DRIVE IS STANDING BY, SIR!
MR. SULU: WARP SPEED!
AYE, SIR...
...WARP SPEED!

NO WAY, KIRK. STANDBY TRANSWARP DRIVE!
AT YOUR COMMAND, SIR!
EXECUTE!
WHAT THE--?
THERE'S "THE GREAT EXPERIMENT," SIR... ADRIFT IN SPACE!
MR. SCOTT, YOU'RE AS GOOD AS YOUR WORD.
AYE, SIR. THE MORE COMPLICATED THE PLUMBIN', THE EASIER IT IS TO STOP UP THE DRAIN.
GENTLEMEN, YOUR WORK TODAY WAS OUTSTANDING. I INTEND TO RECOMMEND YOU ALL FOR PROMOTION...
...IN WHATEVER FLEET WE END UP SERVING.
BEST SPEED TO GENESIS!

LANDING FORCE MATERIALIZED. COMMENCING SEARCH FOR-- AGGGGH!
GROUNDQUAKE! IT--
THIS WAY!
OOOWWWOOOO
THERE IS OUR LIFE-FORM READING! WHAT--?
BEEP BEEP BEEP
MARK

BEWARE, MY LORD! THEY MAY BE--
COWARD!

HSSSSSST..
NOTIFY THE BRIDGE--NOTHING OF CONSEQUENCE HERE.
POPT
SLEEP...

THIS PLANET IS AGING IN SURGES, ISN'T IT? AND SPOCK WITH IT?
THE GENESIS WAVE STARTED A LIFE CLOCK TICKING FOR HIM AND THE PLANET. BUT AT THE RATE THINGS ARE GOING NOW...

HOW LONG WILL IT BE?
DAYS... MAYBE HOURS. THE PROTOMATTER MAKES THE SITUATION UNPREDICTABLE...
...SAAVIK, I'M SOR--

SOMEONE'S COMING.
I'D BETTER SEE WHO IT IS. GIVE ME YOUR PHASER.
BEEP

ESTIMATING ARRIVAL AT GENESIS IN 2.9 HOURS, SIR.
SCAN FOR VESSELS IN PURSUIT.

SCANNING...INDICATIONS NEGATIVE AT THIS TIME.

...DID I DO IT RIGHT...?
YOU DID FINE, BONES... JUST FINE.

HOW WE DOING?
WE ARE DOING FINE... BUT I'D FEEL SAFER GIVING SPOCK ONE OF MY KIDNEYS THAN WHAT'S SCRAMBLED IN MY BRAIN!

ADMIRAL, THERE IS NO RESPONSE FROM THE GRISSOM ON ANY CHANNEL.
KEEP TRYING.

OOOOOOWWWOOOOOOOOOOO

SO IT HAS COME.

YOU FEEL THE BURNING OF YOUR VULCAN BLOOD. IT IS CALLED PON FARR.
...WILL YOU TRUST ME...?

SECURED FROM WARP SPEED, ADMIRAL... NOW ENTERING GENESIS SECTOR OF MUTARA QUADRANT.
STILL NO RESPONSE FROM THE GRISSOM, SIR.

BONES, CAN YOU GIVE ME A QUADRANT BI-SCAN?
...
I THINK YOU JUST EXCEEDED MY CAPABILITIES.

I'LL DO IT, DOCTOR.
SORRY, JIM...
YOUR TIME IS COMING, DOCTOR. MR. SULU, PROCEED AT IMPULSE POWER.

VESSEL ENTERING SECTOR... A FEDERATION CRUISER, CONSTITUTION 2 CLASS!
HAVE THEY SCANNED US?

NOT YET.
ENGAGE CLOAKING DEVICE.

SO! I HAVE COME A LONG WAY FOR THE POWER OF GENESIS! AND WHAT DO I FIND?

A WEAKLING *HUMAN*... A VULCAN *BOY*... AND A *WOMAN*!
MY LORD, WE ARE SURVIVORS OF A DOOMED EXPEDITION! THIS PLANET WILL *DESTROY ITSELF* IN HOURS! THE GENESIS EXPERIMENT IS A *FAILURE*!

A FAILURE? THE MOST DESTRUCTIVE FORCE EVER CREATED! *YOU* WILL TELL ME THE SECRET OF THE GENESIS TORPEDO!
I HAVE NO SUCH KNOWLEDGE.

THEN I HOPE PAIN IS SOMETHING YOU *ENJOY*.
MY LORD, A FEDERATION STARSHIP APPROACHES!

A FEDERATION--?
BRING ME UP! *IMMEDIATELY!*
HMMMMMMMMMMNNNNN

WHAT DID YOU SEE, CHEKOV?
I'D SWEAR IT WAS A SCOUT CLASS VESSEL, SIR... BUT I MIGHT HAVE IMAGINED IT!

IT COULD BE THE GRISSOM... PATCH IN THE HAILING FREQUENCY.
AYE, SIR. GO AHEAD.

GRISSOM, THIS IS ADMIRAL JAMES T. KIRK OF THE USS ENTERPRISE, DO YOU READ?
MY FA--
DAVID, QUIET!

REPORT STATUS!
WE ARE CLOAKED. ENEMY CLOSING ON IMPULSE POWER. RANGE, 5,000 KELLICAMS.
GOOD. THIS IS THE TURN OF LUCK I HAVE BEEN WAITING FOR.

NOTHING ON MY BOARD, SIR.
THERE. THAT DISTORTION. OPINION, SULU?

I THINK IT'S AN ENERGY FORM, SIR.
YES. ENOUGH ENERGY TO CLOAK A SHIP, WOULDN'T YOU SAY? RED ALERT, MR. SCOTT!

ALL POWER TO THE WEAPONS SYSTEMS, SCOTTY!
NO SHIELDS, SIR?

IF MY GUESS IS RIGHT, THEY'LL HAVE TO DE-CLOAK BEFORE THEY CAN FIRE, AND WE'LL HAVE THEM!
MAY ALL YOUR GUESSES BE RIGHT!

500 KELLICAMS!
STANDBY TORPEDOES --DE-CLOAK!

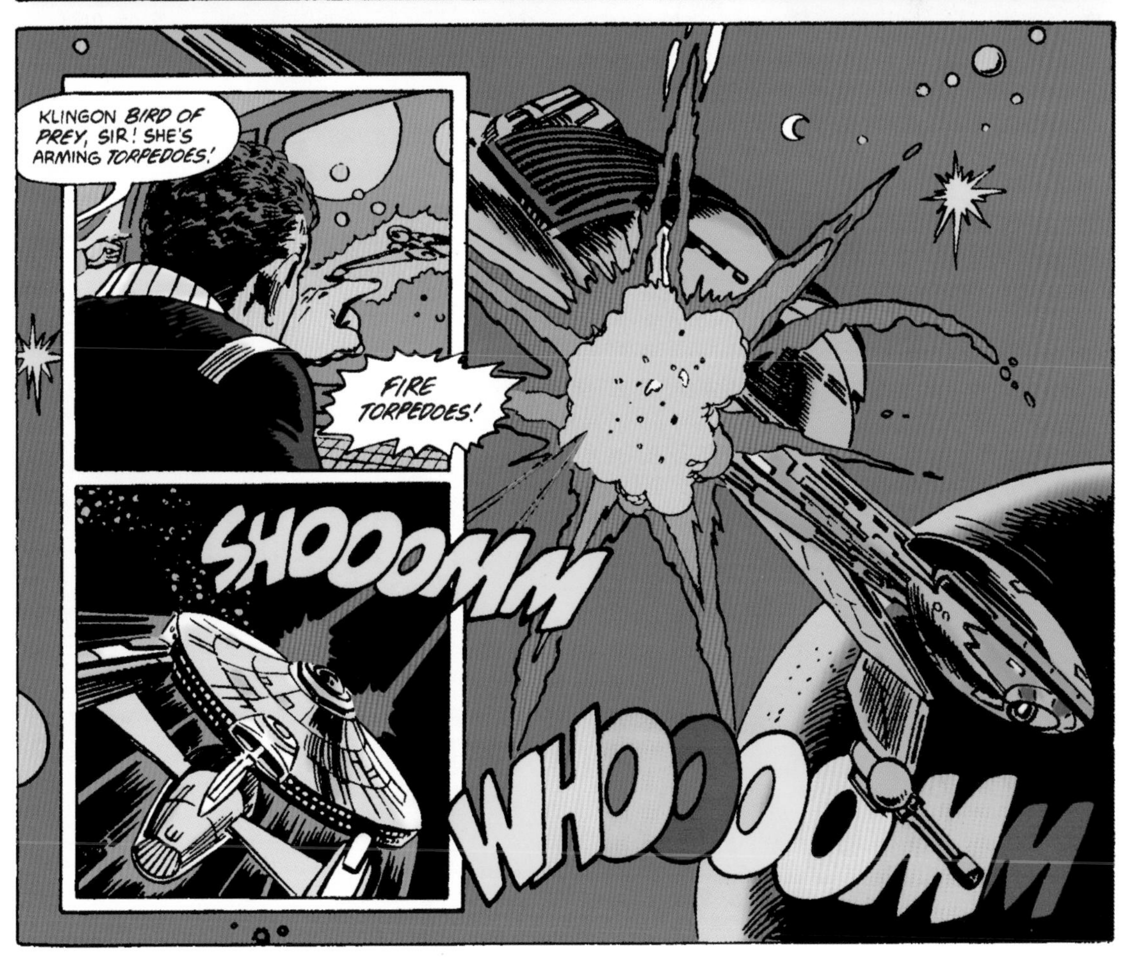
KLINGON BIRD OF PREY, SIR! SHE'S ARMING TORPEDOES!
FIRE TORPEDOES!
SHOOOMM
WHOOOOMM

SIR, THE CLOAKING DEVICE IS DESTROYED!
NEVER MIND...

...EMERGENCY POWER TO THE THRUSTERS! STANDBY WEAPONS!
YES, MY LORD!

FIRE!

NOW, SCOTTY! RAISE SHIELDS!
THE AUTOMATION SYSTEM'S OVERLOADED, SIR! I DINNA EXPECT TO TAKE US INTO COMBAT... WE'VE GOT NO SHIELDS!

FIRE!
CROOOOOMM

MR. SCOTT, TRANSFER EMERGENCY POWER TO THE PHASER BANKS AND SHIELDS--
SIR, I CANNOT!
THEY'VE KNOCKED OUT THE DAMN AUTOMATION CENTER! I'VE GOT NO CONTROL OVER ANYTHING!
SO... WE'RE A SITTING DUCK!
WHY HAVEN'T THEY FINISHED US...?
MY LORD, ENEMY COMMANDER WISHES A TRUCE TO CONFER.
DOES HE? PUT HIM ON THE SCREEN.
COMMANDER, YOUR PRESENCE HERE IS AN ACT OF WAR! YOU HAVE TWO MINUTES TO SURRENDER YOUR VESSEL, OR WE WILL DESTROY YOU!
DO NOT LECTURE ME ABOUT TREATIES! THE FEDERATION, IN CREATING AN ULTIMATE WEAPON, HAS BECOME THE ENEMY OF GALACTIC PEACE!
...ON THE PLANET BELOW, I HAVE THREE PRISONERS WHO HELPED DEVELOP YOUR DOOMSDAY WEAPON. SURRENDER IMMEDIATELY, OR I WILL EXECUTE THEM!
I DEMAND TO SPEAK TO THEM!
ADMIRAL KIRK, THIS IS LT. SAAVIK. DR. DAVID MARCUS IS HERE, AND A VULCAN SCIENTIST OF YOUR ACQUAINTANCE.
THIS VULCAN... IS HE ALIVE?

HE IS NOT HIMSELF, BUT HE LIVES. HE IS SUBJECT TO RAPID AGING--LIKE THIS UNSTABLE PLANET.
LET ME SPEAK TO DAVID.

DAVID... SORRY I'M LATE.
I'M SORRY, SIR. GENESIS DOESN'T WORK. DON'T SURRENDER! THEY WON'T KILL US FOR--
ENOUGH!

ADMIRAL KIRK, YOUR YOUNG FRIEND IS MISTAKEN; I AM GOING TO KILL ONE OF THE PRISONERS.
WAIT! GIVE ME A CHANCE--
SERGEANT KNORR, KILL ONE OF THEM. I DON'T CARE WHICH.

YOU! THE WOMAN--!
NO!

AGGGH...!

THIS IS SAAVIK, ADMIRAL... DAVID IS DEAD.

YOU KLINGON BASTARD...!
YOU'VE KILLED MY SON!

HAVE I? SURRENDER YOUR VESSEL, ADMIRAL, OR THE OTHER TWO WILL DIE.
ALL RIGHT, DAMN YOU! GIVE ME A MINUTE TO INFORM MY CREW.

I GIVE YOU TWO MINUTES. BIRD OF PREY OUT.
MR. SULU, WHAT IS THE CREW COMPLIMENT OF A BIRD OF PREY?
ABOUT A DOZEN OFFICERS AND MEN, SIR, BUT--

THEN I SWEAR TO YOU, WE'RE NOT FINISHED YET!
WE NEVER HAVE BEEN, JIM!

BONES, YOU AND SULU TO THE TRANSPORTER ROOM.
MR. SCOTT, MR. CHEKOV, WITH ME. WE HAVE A FINAL JOB TO DO.

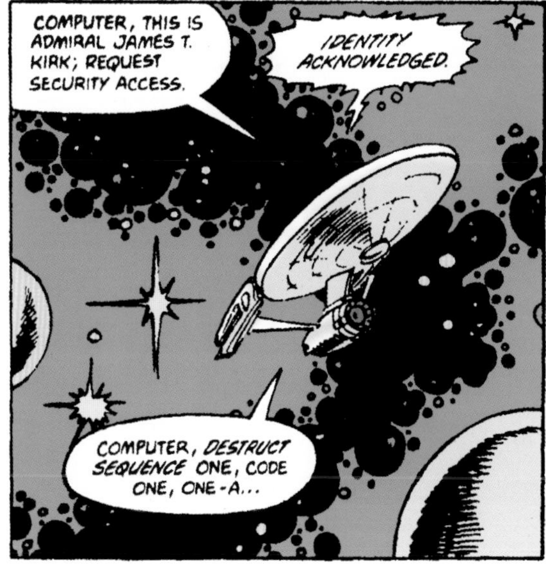
COMPUTER, THIS IS ADMIRAL JAMES T. KIRK; REQUEST SECURITY ACCESS.
IDENTITY ACKNOWLEDGED.
COMPUTER, DESTRUCT SEQUENCE ONE, CODE ONE, ONE-A...

TO THE TRANSPORTER ROOM! ONCE YOU CONTROL THE SHIP, WE WILL TAKE THE SECRET OF GENESIS FROM THEIR OWN MEMORY BANKS! SUCCESS!
SUCCESS!

...COMMANDER CHEKOV, ACTING SCIENCE OFFICER: DESTRUCT SEQUENCE TWO, CODE ONE, ONE-A, TWO-B.
...COMMANDER SCOTT, CHIEF ENGINEERING OFFICER: DESTRUCT SEQUENCE THREE, CODE ONE-B, TWO-B, THREE.
AWAITING FINAL CODE FOR ONE-MINUTE COUNTDOWN.

CODE ZERO, ZERO, ZERO DESTRUCT ZERO.
ONE MINUTE... FIFTY-NINE SECONDS... FIFTY-EIGHT...

...FIFTY-SEVEN... FIFTY-SIX...
ADMIRAL, WE'VE NOT MUCH TIME...
I'M AWARE OF THAT, MR. SCOTT...

...I JUST WANTED... ONE LAST LOOK.
...FIFTY-FIVE...

REMOTE COMMAND-- ENERGIZE.
HMMMMMMMMMNNN

HMMMMMMMMNNN

MY LORD, THE SHIP APPEARS TO BE DESERTED.
CHECK THE BRIDGE.
SIR, THE BRIDGE APPEARS TO BE RUN BY COMPUTER. DO YOU HEAR IT?
NINE... EIGHT... SEVEN...

SIX... FIVE... FOUR...
GET OUT OF THERE! GET OUT!
...THREE...
... TWO...
...ONE...

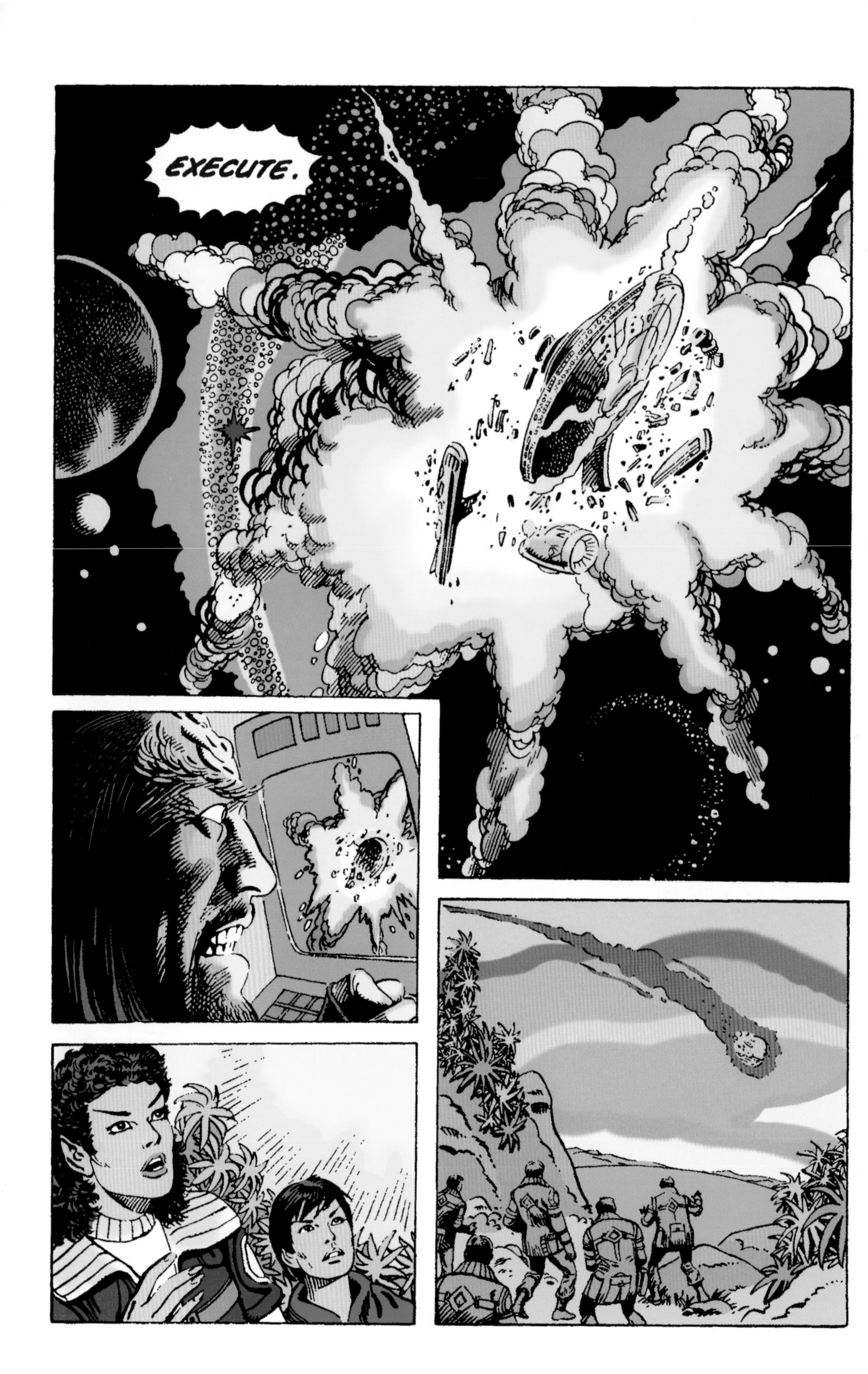
EXECUTE.

MY GOD, BONES... WHAT HAVE I DONE?
WHAT YOU HAD TO DO. WHAT YOU ALWAYS DO! TURN DEATH INTO A FIGHTING CHANCE TO LIVE!

YOU HEAR ME, JIM?
YES, DOCTOR... THANK YOU.
SIR, PLANET CORE READINGS ARE HIGHLY UNSTABLE, CHANGING RAPIDLY...

SURFACE LIFE-SIGNS?
CLOSE, ADMIRAL... THAT WAY.
COME ON.

MY LORD... WHAT ARE YOUR ORDERS?
HE DESTROYED HIMSELF... THE ONE THING I DIDN'T ANTICIPATE... A HUMAN HAS BEEN BOLDER, MORE RUTHLESS THAN I... THAT IS THE REAL DISHONOR!

LORD COMMANDER, THIS PLACE IS BREAKING UP... RECOMMEND BEAMING UP OURSELVES AND THE PRISONERS...

WHAT'S WRONG WITH HIM?
NO, DON'T TOUCH HIM!

WHAT--?

SNAPPP
BY KAHLESS--!

YOU'LL PAY FOR--
DON'T MOVE!

WHREE
EEE
BONES, TEND TO SPOCK!

OH, ADMIRAL...
EASY, SAAVIK, IT'S ALL RIGHT...

...IT'S ALL--
MY GOD...

...DAVID...

MY SON... "TO THEE NO STAR BE DARK... BOTH HEAVEN AND EARTH... FRIEND THEE FOREVER..."
JIM!

HOW IS HE, BONES?
HE'S AGING RAPIDLY... ALL GENETIC FUNCTIONS ARE HIGHLY ACCELERATED.
AND HIS MIND?

HIS MIND'S A VOID. IT WOULD SEEM, ADMIRAL, THAT I'VE GOT ALL HIS MARBLES!
IS THERE ANYTHING WE CAN DO?
GET HIM OFF THIS PLANET, SIR.

OFF THIS PLANET? BUT HOW, I-- WAIT!
KLINGON COMMANDER, THIS IS KIRK! I HAVE THE SECRET OF GENESIS, BUT YOU'LL HAVE TO BRING US UP THERE TO GET IT... DO YOU HEAR ME?

DO YOU HEAR ME? I--
DROP ALL WEAPONS!

MALTZ, PRISONERS ARE AT COORDINATES. *ACTIVATE BEAM!*
YOU SHOULD TAKE THE VULCAN, TOO.

NO.
WHY NOT?
BECAUSE YOU *WISH* IT.

GENESIS. I *WANT* IT.
YOU FOOL, LOOK *AROUND* YOU! THIS PLANET IS *DESTROYING ITSELF!*

YES! EXHILARATING, ISN'T IT?
IF WE DON'T *HELP* EACH OTHER, WE'LL ALL *DIE* HERE!

PERFECT! THAT'S THE WAY IT SHALL *BE!*
CCCCRAKKKKKKKKK

KPPRCC

DON'T BE A FOOL--
GIVE ME YOUR HAND!
SAVED? BY YOU...?

NO!

I HAVE HAD... ENOUGH OF YOU!
YAAAAAAAAAAaaa

SPOCK...?

SPOCK!
"GET HIM OFF THIS PLANET," SAAVIK SAID. BUT HOW--?

MALTZ, THIS IS YOUR COMMANDER! KIRK IS DEAD, ACTIVATE BEAM!

YOUR ADMIRAL IS DEAD, AND GENESIS IS OURS! WE HAVE WON!

SORRY, BUT WHERE DEATH IS CONCERNED, I DON'T PLAY FAIR!
BONES, TAKE SPOCK! EVERYONE ELSE, STATIONS! MALTZ, HELP US OR DIE!
I... I DO NOT DESERVE TO LIVE!

FINE, I'LL KILL YOU LATER!
GENTLEMEN, LET'S GET OUT OF HERE!

ANYONE HERE READ KLINGONESE?
NOT ME, ADMIRAL!
NO, SIR.
NO, ADMIRAL.
I DO NOT.
WELL, TAKE YOUR BEST SHOT.
IF VE CAN BYPASS INTO THIS MODULE--
FINE, BUT WHERE'S THE DAMN ANTI-MATTER INDUCER?
THIS? NO, THIS!
THIS OR NOTHIN'...!
IF I READ THIS RIGHT, SIR, WE HAVE FULL POWER!
THERE'S ONLY ONE WAY TO FIND OUT! GO, SULU!
MY CONGRATULATIONS ON YOUR READING EXPERTISE, MR. SULU.

GOOD-BYE, DAVID.

BEST SPEED TO VULCAN, MR. SULU. MR. CHEKOV, TAKE THE PRISONER BELOW.
YOU SAID YOU WOULD KILL ME!
I LIED.

MR. SAAVIK, MESSAGE TO AMBASSADOR SAREK: TELL HIM WE BRING McCOY AND A LIVING SPOCK. ASK HIM TO PREPARE FOR THE KATRA RITUAL.
YES, ADMIRAL; BUT THAT MAY NOT BE POSSIBLE.
WHAT?

THE KATRA RITUAL IS MEANT TO DEPOSIT SPOCK'S CONSCIOUSNESS IN THE HALL OF ANCIENT THOUGHT... NOT IN HIS BODY.
BUT--
WHAT YOU DESCRIBE IS CALLED FAL TOR PAN... "THE REFUSION."

IT IS VERY DANGEROUS. THE ELDERS MAY CHOOSE NOT TO ATTEMPT IT.
AND IF THEY DON'T? WHAT WILL HAPPEN TO SPOCK...?

"...HE WILL REMAIN ALWAYS AS HE IS NOW..."

SPOCK, I'VE DONE EVERYTHING I KNOW TO DO... PLEASE, HELP ME!
YOU STUCK ME WITH IT, FOR GOD'S SAKE, TEACH ME WHAT TO DO WITH IT!

I NEVER THOUGHT I'D SAY THIS TO YOU... BUT I'VE MISSED YOU...
...AND I COULDN'T BEAR TO LOSE YOU AGAIN...

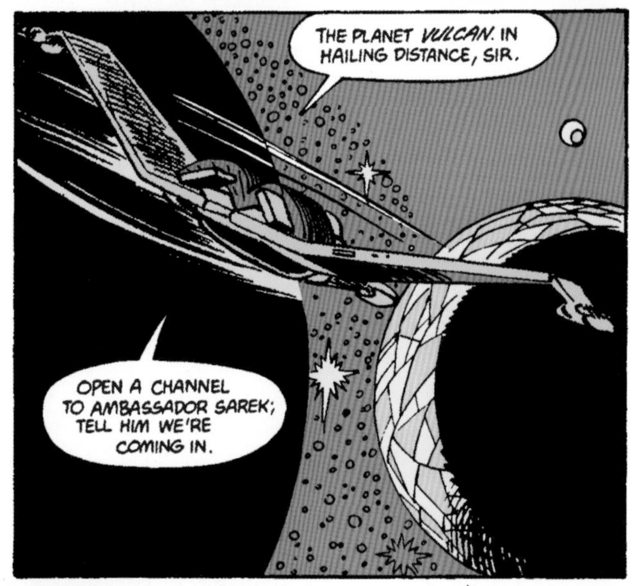
THE PLANET VULCAN. IN HAILING DISTANCE, SIR.
OPEN A CHANNEL TO AMBASSADOR SAREK; TELL HIM WE'RE COMING IN.

ADMIRAL KIRK REQUESTING PERMISSION TO LAND, SIR.
PERMISSION GRANTED. TELL HIM WE ARE READY.

MR. SULU, YOU'RE ON MANUAL.
IT'S BEEN A WHILE, SIR... HERE WE GO...!
FIRE RETROTHRUSTERS!

WE'RE DOWN, SIR.
BONES, LET'S GET SPOCK OFF-LOADED!

MY GOD...!

THE FAL TOR PAN IS NOT ATTEMPTED LIGHTLY, ADMIRAL... MUCH IS AT STAKE.
ADMIRAL!

SAREK IS WAITING ABOVE... MAY I HELP?
OF COURSE.

LIVE LONG AND PROSPER, SPOCK ...

SAREK, DO YOU SENSE *ANY*--

ONLY THE RITUAL OF *FAL TOR PAN* CAN REJOIN HIS BODY AND HIS MIND, KIRK... *IF* THE ELDERS PERMIT IT.

YOUR FRIENDS WILL WAIT HERE, KIRK. YOU AND McCOY WILL FOLLOW.

SAREK, CHILD OF SKON, CHILD OF SOLKAR: THE BODY OF THY SON BREATHES STILL. WHAT IS THY WISH?
I ASK FOR FAL TOR PAN, THE REFUSION.

WHAT THEE SEEK HAS NOT BEEN DONE SINCE AGES PAST--AND THEN, ONLY IN LEGEND. THY REQUEST IS NOT LOGICAL.
FORGIVE ME, T'LAR. MY LOGIC FALTERS WHERE MY SON IS CONCERNED.
WHO IS THE KEEPER OF THE KATRA?

I AM... McCOY, LEONARD H... SON OF DAVID...
McCOY, WITH THY APPROVAL, WE SHALL USE ALL OUR POWERS TO RETURN TO SPOCK'S BODY THAT WHICH THEE POSSESS: HIS ESSENCE. BUT, McCOY..

...BE WARNED: THE DANGER TO THYSELF IS AS GRAVE AS THE DANGER TO SPOCK. THEE MUST MAKE THE CHOICE.
I CHOOSE THE DANGER.

ALL THAT CAN BE DONE... SHALL BE DONE...

...THOUGH IT TAKES FULL TURN OF THE VULCAN SUN...

... STRANGEST DREAM, I--

BONES...?

I'M... I'M ALL RIGHT, JIM.
WHAT ABOUT SPOCK?
I AM NOT SURE. ONLY TIME WILL ANSWER.

KIRK, I THANK YOU. WHAT YOU HAVE DONE IS--
WHAT I HAVE DONE, I HAD TO DO
BUT AT WHAT COST? YOUR SHIP... YOUR SON...

IF I HADN'T TRIED, THE COST WOULD HAVE BEEN MY SOUL.
UNDERSTOOD.

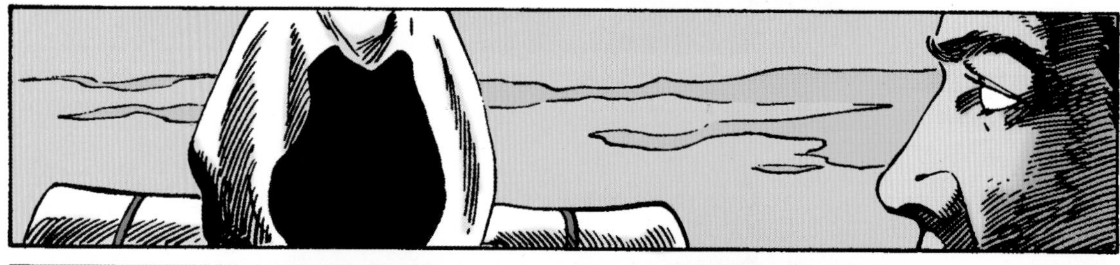

I KNOW YOU... DO I NOT?
YES. AND I, YOU.
MY FATHER SAYS YOU HAVE BEEN MY FRIEND... YOU CAME BACK FOR ME.

YOU WOULD HAVE DONE THE SAME FOR ME.
WHY WOULD YOU DO THIS...?

BECAUSE... THE NEEDS OF THE ONE OUTWEIGHED THE NEEDS OF THE MANY.

"I HAVE BEEN... AND ALWAYS SHALL BE... YOUR FRIEND..."
YES, YES, SPOCK...

THE SHIP... OUT OF DANGER...?
YOU SAVED THE SHIP, SPOCK. YOU SAVED US ALL. DON'T YOU REMEMBER?

...JIM...
...YOUR NAME IS JIM.

...YES! WELCOME BACK, SPOCK...

...WELCOME BACK...MY FRIEND!
"You belong at your captain's side, Mr. Spock... as if you've always been there, and always will."
--Edith Keeler, CITY ON THE EDGE OF FOREVER

ART BY DAVID DIETRICK

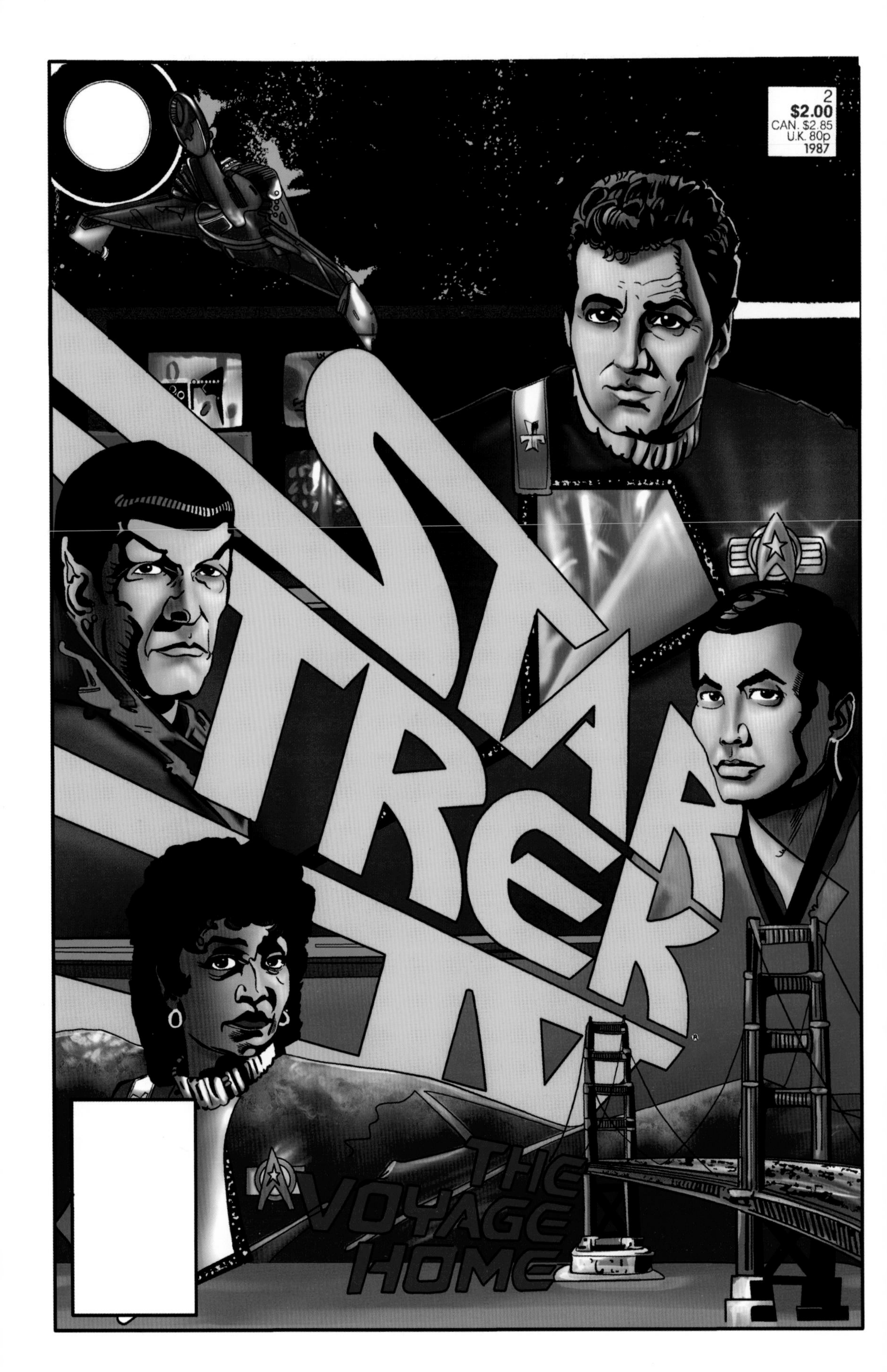
2
$2.00
CAN. $2.85
U.K. 80p
1987
STAR TREK
THE VOYAGE HOME

ADAPTED BY MIKE W. BARR • WRITER
TOM SUTTON & RICARDO VILLAGRÁN • ARTISTS
AGUSTIN MAS • MICHELE WOLFMAN
LETTERER COLORIST
ROBERT GREENBERGER • EDITOR.
UFP
UFP

SCIENCE OFFICER, WHAT DO YOU MAKE OF IT?
IT APPEARS TO BE A PROBE, CAPTAIN, FROM AN INTELLIGENCE UNKNOWN TO US.

CONTINUE TRANSMITTING; UNIVERSAL PEACE AND HELLO IN ALL KNOWN LANGUAGES. COMMUNICATIONS, GET ME STARFLEET COMMAND.
AYE, SIR.
YES, CAPTAIN.

GO AHEAD, CAPTAIN.
STARFLEET COMMAND, THIS IS USS SARATOGA, PATROLLING SECTOR 5, NEUTRAL ZONE. WE ARE TRACKING A PROBE OF UNKNOWN ORIGIN ON APPARENT TRAJECTORY TO THE TERRAN SOLAR SYSTEM. ATTEMPTS TO COMMUNICATE HAVE BEEN NEGATIVE.

CONTINUE TRACKING, SARATOGA. WE WILL ANALYZE TRANSMISSIONS AND ADVISE.
ROGER, STARFLEET. SARATOGA OUT.
RANGE 400,000 KILOMETERS, CLOSING... CAPTAIN, HERE COMES THEIR SIGNAL AGAIN...

IS THEIR SIGNAL CAUSING OUR POWER DRAIN?
I THINK SO, CAPTAIN; IT'S BEING CARRIED ON AN AMPLIFICATION WAVE OF ENORMOUS POWER!
MRAAAWNNKKK

EMERGENCY THRUSTERS!
MRAAAWNNNKKKK
NO RESPONSE, CAPTAIN-- WE'RE ON RESERVE POWER ONLY, AND THAT THING'S ON A COLLISION COURSE!

ALL HANDS, RIG FOR COLLISION...
MRAAAWWWWKKKK

MRAAAWW
EMERGENCY POWER!

WKKKK
EMERGENCY--!

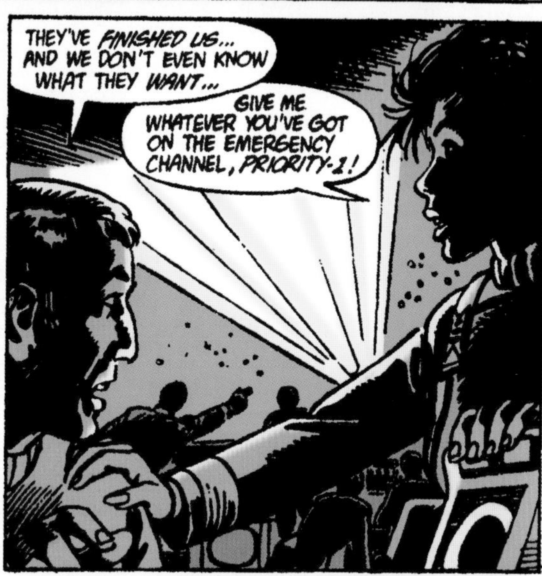
THEY'VE FINISHED US... AND WE DON'T EVEN KNOW WHAT THEY WANT...
GIVE ME WHATEVER YOU'VE GOT ON THE EMERGENCY CHANNEL, PRIORITY-1!

THANK YOU FOR COMING, AMBASSADOR SAREK. IT'S NOT GOING WELL.
AM I TOO LATE TO TESTIFY, DR. CHAPEL?
I DON'T KNOW.
COUNCIL
FEDERATION OF PLANETS

THERE! YOU SEE THE DESTRUCTION OF WHICH THE FEDERATION IS CAPABLE...!

AND BEHOLD THE IMAGE OF THE QUINTES-SENTIAL DEVIL IN THESE MATTERS-- JAMES T. KIRK, RENEGADE AND TERRORIST!
NOT ONLY IS HE RESPONSIBLE FOR THE MURDER OF A KLINGON CREW, AND THE THEFT OF A KLINGON VESSEL...

...BUT EVEN AS THE FEDERATION SPOKE OF PEACE, KIRK WAS SECRETELY DEVELOPING NOT ONLY THE GENESIS TORPEDO...
GENESIS DEVICE

...BUT THE EUPHEMISTICALLY-TITLED "GENESIS PLANET"--A SECRET BASE FROM WHICH TO LAUNCH THE ANNIHILATION OF THE KLINGON PEOPLE!

MR. PRESIDENT, WE DEMAND THE EXTRADITION OF KIRK! WE DEMAND JUSTICE!
KLINGON JUSTICE IS-- EUPHEMISTICALLY PUT--A UNIQUE POINT OF VIEW, MR. PRESIDENT...

GENESIS WAS PERFECTLY NAMED: THE CREATION OF *LIFE*, NOT DEATH. IT WAS THE KLINGONS WHO SHED FIRST BLOOD TRYING TO POSSESS ITS SECRETS.
VULCANS ARE WELL-KNOWN AS THE INTELLEC-TUAL *PUPPETS* OF THE FEDERATION!

YOUR VESSEL DID DESTROY *USS GRISSOM*. YOUR MEN DID KILL KIRK'S SON. DO YOU DENY THESE EVENTS?
WE DENY NOTHING! WE HAVE THE RIGHT TO PRESERVE OUR RACE!

DO YOU HAVE THE RIGHT TO MURDER?

ORDER. THERE WILL BE NO FURTHER OUTBURSTS FROM THE FLOOR.
MR. PRESIDENT, I HAVE COME TO SPEAK ON BEHALF OF THE ACCUSED.
PERSONAL BIAS! HIS SON WAS SAVED BY KIRK!

AMBASSADOR SAREK, WITH ALL RESPECT, THE COUNCIL'S DELIBERATIONS ARE OVER. YOU HAVE BEEN ALLOWED TO SPEAK IN ORDER TO PUT YOUR VIEWS ON THE RECORD.
THEN KIRK GOES *UNPUNISHED*?

ADMIRAL KIRK *HAS* BEEN CHARGED WITH NINE VIOLATIONS OF STARFLEET REGULATIONS--
STARFLEET REGULATIONS? OUTRAGOUS! REMEMBER THIS *WELL*...

THERE WILL BE NO PEACE AS LONG AS KIRK LIVES!

=SIGH= SAREK OF VULCAN, WITH ALL RESPECT--WE ASK YOU TO RETURN KIRK AND HIS CREW TO ANSWER FOR THEIR CRIMES.
WITH RESPECT TO YOU, MR. PRESIDENT, THERE IS ONLY ONE CRIME:

"...DENYING KIRK AND HIS CREW THE HONORS THEY SO RICHLY DESERVE."
CAPTAIN'S LOG, STARDATE 8390...

...WE ARE IN THE THIRD MONTH OF OUR VULCAN EXILE, AND IT WAS DR. McCOY, WITH A FINE SENSE OF HISTORICAL IRONY...

...WHO DECIDED ON A NAME FOR OUR CAPTURED KLINGON VESSEL.
HMS BOUNTY
LET THE RECORD SHOW...

...THAT THE COMMANDER AND CREW OF THE LATE STARSHIP ENTERPRISE HAVE VOTED UNANIMOUSLY TO RETURN TO EARTH TO FACE THE CONSEQUENCES OF THEIR ACTIONS.
THANK YOU ALL... REPAIR STATIONS, PLEASE.

MR. SCOTT, HOW SOON CAN WE GET UNDERWAY?
GIVE ME ONE MORE DAY, SIR. THE DAMAGE CONTROL IS EASY, IT'S READIN' *KLINGON* THAT'S HARD.
BAD *ENOUGH* TO BE COURT-MARTIALLED AND SPEND THE REST OF OUR LIVES MINING BORITE...

...BUT TO COME HOME IN THIS *FLEA TRAP*--
WE COULD LEARN A THING OR TWO FROM THIS "FLEA TRAP," DOCTOR. IT HAS A CLOAKING DEVICE THAT'S SECOND TO NONE.
ADMIRAL...?

...HERE IS A DEPOSITION I HAVE MADE. IF IT IS NOT SUFFICIENT--
DON'T CONCERN YOURSELF, SAAVIK; YOUR LEAVE HAS BEEN GRANTED FOR GOOD AND PROPER CAUSE. HOW ARE YOU FEELING?

I AM WELL, ADMIRAL.

YOU'LL BE IN GOOD HANDS HERE.

RESUME?
RESUME MEMORY TESTING.

WHO SAID: LOGIC IS THE CEMENT OF OUR CIVILIZATION AS WE ASCEND FROM CHAOS, USING REASON AS OUR GUIDE?
T'PLANA-HATH, MATRON OF VULCAN PHILOSOPHY.

WHAT WAS KIRI-KIN-THA'S FIRST LAW OF METAPHYSICS?
NOTHING THAT IS UNREAL MAY EXIST.

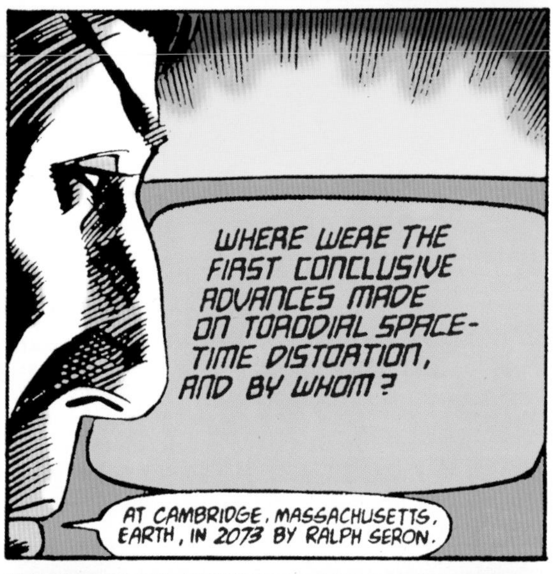
WHERE WERE THE FIRST CONCLUSIVE ADVANCES MADE ON TOROIDAL SPACE-TIME DISTORTION, AND BY WHOM?
AT CAMBRIDGE, MASSACHUSETTS, EARTH, IN 2073 BY RALPH SERON.

MEMORY TEST SATISFACTORY. READY FOR FINAL QUESTION?
AFFIRMATIVE.

HOW DO YOU FEEL?
?

I ...I DO NOT UNDERSTAND...
...I DO NOT UNDERSTAND THE FINAL QUESTION.
YOU ARE HALF-HUMAN. THE COMPUTER KNOWS THAT.
THE QUESTION IS IRRELEVANT, MOTHER. I HAVE NO FEELINGS.
SPOCK... DOES THE GOOD OF THE MANY OUTWEIGH THE GOOD OF THE ONE?
I WOULD ACCEPT THAT AS SELF-EVIDENT.
THEN YOU STAND HERE ALIVE BECAUSE OF A MISTAKE, MADE BY YOUR FLAWED, FEELING HUMAN FRIENDS. THEY HAVE SACRIFICED THEIR FUTURES BECAUSE THEY BELIEVED THE GOOD OF THE ONE--YOU--WAS MORE IMPORTANT TO THEM.
HUMANS OFTEN MAKE ILLOGICAL DECISIONS.
MRAAAWWWWKKKK
STATUS REPORT, ADMIRAL CARTWRIGHT.

MR. PRESIDENT, THE PROBE IS HEADED TOWARD EARTH. IT'S SOMEHOW NEUTRALIZING EVERY VESSEL IT MEETS.

DID THEY REACH A DECISION ABOUT JIM AND THE OTHERS, CHRIS?
NO, JANICE, THIS STRANGE "PROBE" HAS TAKEN PRIORITY.
THE PROBE USES SOME KIND OF ENERGY WE JUST DON'T UNDERSTAND, SIR.
CAN YOU PROTECT US?
"I--I'M NOT SURE, SIR. WE'RE LAUNCHING EVERYTHING WE HAVE."
EXCELSIOR AND INTREPID ARE CLEARED TO DEPART...
...OPEN SPACEDOCK DOORS.
SIR! SPACEDOCK DOORS ARE INOPERATIVE!
INTREPID TO CONTROL. ARE UNABLE TO DEPART; HAVE SOMEHOW LOST ALL POWER!
WHAT'S GOING ON HERE!
MRRAAAWWWKKK

STARFLEET COMMAND, THIS IS SPACEDOCK ON EMERGENCY CHANNEL. WE HAVE LOST ALL INTERNAL POWER, REPEAT...
MRAAAWWWNKKKK
MRAAAWWWWNKKK
WHAT THE DEVIL? WHERE DID THIS FOG SPRING UP FROM?
STATION REPORTS SAY CLOUD COVER IS INCREASING ALL OVER THE WORLD, SIR...
"...WE THINK IT'S THE WORK OF THE PROBE..."
SYSTEMS REPORT. COMMUNICATIONS?
COMMUNICATIONS SYSTEMS READY, ADMIRAL...

...COMMUNICATIONS OFFICER... READY AS SHE'LL EVER BE.
UNDERSTOOD.
MR. SULU?

GUIDANCE IS FUNCTIONAL, SIR. I'VE ACCESSED THE FEDERATION MEMORY BANKS, AND ONBOARD COMPUTER WILL INTERFACE.
GOOD WORK, SULU. WEAPONS SYSTEMS, MR. CHEKOV?

OPERATIONAL, ADMIRAL. CLOAKING DEVICE NOW AVAILABLE IN ALL MODES OF FLIGHT. WE ARE IN AN ENEMY VESSEL, AFTER ALL.
MOST PRUDENT.

ENGINE ROOM IS READY, SIR, AND I'VE REPLACED THE KLINGON FOOD PACKS. THEY WERE GIVIN' ME A SOUR STOMACH.
APPRECIATED BY ALL, MR. SCOTT. PREPARE FOR DEPARTURE.

WELL, SAAVIK, I GUESS THIS IS GOODBYE. HOW DO YOU FEEL?
FINE, ADMIRAL... SIR...

YOUR SON... DAVID DIED MOST BRAVELY. HE SAVED SPOCK. HE SAVED US ALL. I THOUGHT YOU SHOULD KNOW.
THANK YOU.

GOOD DAY, CAPTAIN SPOCK. MAY YOUR JOURNEY BE FREE OF INCIDENT.
LIVE LONG AND PROSPER, LIEUTENANT.

PERMISSION TO COME ABOARD, ADMIRAL.
PERMISSION GRANTED, SPOCK... BUT MY NAME IS JIM... REMEMBER?

IT WOULD BE IMPROPER TO REFER TO YOU BY THAT NAME WHILE YOU ARE IN COMMAND, ADMIRAL. ALSO I MUST APOLOGIZE FOR MY ATTIRE...
...I SEEM TO HAVE MISPLACED MY UNIFORM.
I... FIND THAT UNDERSTANDABLE, SPOCK. YOU'VE BEEN THROUGH A LOT.

JIM, ARE YOU SURE THIS IS SUCH A BRIGHT IDEA? SPOCK ISN'T EXACTLY WORKING ON ALL THRUSTERS.
IT'LL COME BACK TO HIM, BONES.

ARE YOU SURE?
THAT'S WHAT I THOUGHT.

MR. SULU... TAKE US HOME.
VROOOOOM

ESTIMATE 93.2% CLOUD COVER. TEMPERATURES DROPPING RAPIDLY. NO WAY KNOWN TO DISSIPATE CLOUD COVER.
ADMIRAL...?
SWITCH POWER TO PLANETARY RESERVES.

MR. PRESIDENT, EVEN WITH PLANETARY RESERVES, WE CANNOT SURVIVE WITHOUT THE SUN.
I AM WELL AWARE OF THAT, ADMIRAL.

SAREK... IS THERE NO ANSWER WE CAN GIVE THIS PROBE?
IT IS DIFFICULT TO ANSWER IF ONE DOES NOT UNDERSTAND THE QUESTION.
MRAAAWWWWWWRRR

NO, ADMIRAL, NO SIGNS OF FEDERATION ESCORT. IN FACT, I READ NO FEDERATION VESSELS ON ASSIGNED PATROL STATIONS.
ODD. UHURA, WHAT'S ON THE COMM CHANNELS?

MULTI-PHASIC TRANSMISSIONS, SIR... OVERLAPPING... LET ME SEE IF I CAN SORT IT OUT.
PERHAPS MY ASSISTANCE MAY BE OF USE.

HI... YOU BUSY?
UHURA IS BUSY. I AM MONITORING.

WELL, IT'S NICE TO HAVE YOUR KATRA BACK IN YOUR HEAD, NOT MINE. I MAY HAVE CARRIED YOUR SOUL, BUT I SURE COULDN'T FILL YOUR SHOES.
STARFLEET PROVIDES APPROPRIATE FOOTWEAR FOR ALL PERSONNEL.

SPOCK, OUR EXPERIENCE WAS UNIQUE! CAN'T YOU TELL ME WHAT IT FELT LIKE?
DISCUSSION OF THE SUBJECT WITHOUT A COMMON FRAME OF REFERENCE IS IMPOSSIBLE.

YOU MEAN I HAVE TO DIE TO DISCUSS YOUR INSIGHTS ON DEATH?
PARDON ME, DOCTOR; I AM HEARING MANY CALLS OF DISTRESS.

ADMIRAL, I'M PICKING UP A TRANSMISSION FROM EARTH... THE FEDERATION PRESIDENT...
ON SCREEN.

ALL STARSHIPS... DO NOT APPROACH PLANET EARTH! ORBITING PROBE EMITS WAVE... DIRECTED AT OCEANS...NULLIFIED ALL POWER SOURCES...
CLOUDS ENVELOP PLANET... TORRENTIAL GLOBAL RAINS...PROBE IGNORES ALL OUR RESPONSES... SAVE YOURSELVES... FAREWELL...

UHURA, CAN YOU PICK UP THIS PROBE'S TRANSMISSIONS?
I THINK... YES, SIR--ON SPEAKERS.

MRAAAAWWWKKKK
SPOCK, WHAT DO YOU MAKE OF IT?
MOST UNUSUAL; AN UNKNOWN FORM OF ENERGY, OBVIOUSLY OF GREAT POWER. IT IS LOGICAL TO ASSUME IT IS THE PRODUCT OF A GREAT INTELLIGENCE.

FURTHERMORE, IF SUCH POWER WISHED TO DESTROY US, IT WOULD HAVE. ITS INTENTIONS MAY NOT BE HOSTILE.
OH? YOU THINK THIS IS ITS WAY OF SAYING "HI" TO US EARTHLINGS?

THERE ARE OTHER INTELLIGENT LIFE FORMS ON EARTH, DOCTOR. ONLY HUMAN ARROGANCE WOULD ASSUME THE MESSAGE WAS MEANT FOR MAN.
I LIKED HIM BETTER BEFORE HE DIED.

SPOCK... YOU'RE SUGGESTING THE TRANSMISSION IS MEANT FOR A LIFE FORM OTHER THAN MAN?
IT IS AT LEAST A POSSIBILITY, CAPTAIN. THE PRESIDENT DID SAY THE TRANSMISSION WAS DIRECTED AT EARTH'S OCEANS.

SO HE DID... UHURA, CAN YOU MODIFY THE PROBE'S SIGNAL, ACCOUNTING FOR DENSITY OF WATER, TEMPERATURE AND SALINITY FACTORS?
I'LL TRY... I THINK I HAVE IT, SIR...

REEEKT-REEEKT!
SPOCK, WHERE ARE YOU GOING?
TO THE COMPUTER CENTER. IF MY SUPPOSITION IS CORRECT, THERE CAN BE NO RESPONSE TO THIS MESSAGE.

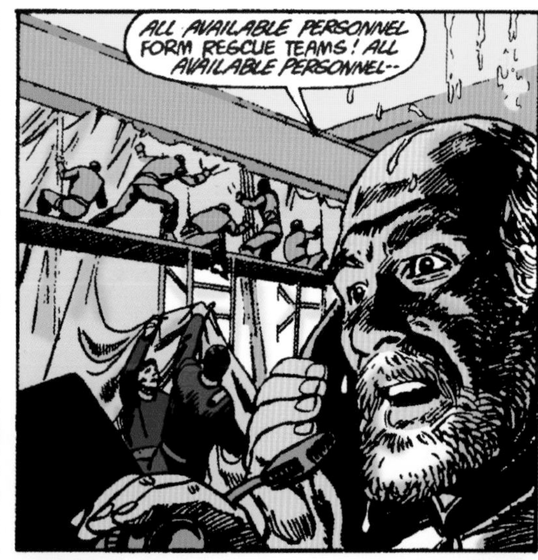
ALL AVAILABLE PERSONNEL FORM RESCUE TEAMS! ALL AVAILABLE PERSONNEL--

SPOCK, WHAT HAVE YOU FOUND?
AS SUSPECTED, ADMIRAL, THE PROBE'S TRANSMISSIONS ARE--SOMEWHAT MODIFIED--THE SONGS SUNG BY HUMPBACK WHALES.

IT'S POSSIBLE... WHALES EXISTED LONG BEFORE MAN...
10 MILLION YEARS EARLIER. HUMPBACKS HAVE BEEN EXTINCT SINCE THE 21 ST CENTURY... THE PROBE MAY HAVE BEEN SENT TO CONTACT THEM.

BUT... THERE WON'T BE AN ANSWER...
SPOCK, COULD THE ANSWER TO THIS CALL-- THE WHALESONG--BE SIMULATED?
THE SOUNDS, BUT NOT THE LANGUAGE.

WE WOULD BE RESPONDING IN GIBBERISH. UNFORTUNATELY, THE HUMPBACK WHALE WAS INDIGENOUS ONLY TO EARTH. EARTH OF THE PAST.
THEN WE MUST DESTROY THE PROBE BEFORE IT DESTROYS EARTH.

ILLOGICAL, ADMIRAL. THE PROBE HAS NEUTRALIZED STARSHIPS; WE WOULD FARE NO BETTER.
BLAST IT, SPOCK, WE CAN'T JUST TURN AWAY! THERE'S GOT TO BE AN ALTERNATIVE!

WE COULD ATTEMPT TO FIND SOME HUMPBACK WHALES.
BUT THEY'RE EXTINCT!
IN THE PRESENT, YES...

"IN THE PRESENT"? WAIT JUST A DAMN MINUTE--
SPOCK, START YOUR COMPUTATIONS FOR THE SLINGSHOT TIME WARP EFFECT. BONES, LET'S PAY SCOTTY A VISIT.

ADMIRAL, THESE WHALE BEASTIES WEIGH 20 TONS OR SO EACH. HOW'LL WE HANDLE ALL THAT WEIGHT?
YOU'LL WORK IT OUT, SCOTTY. AND REMEMBER, THERE WILL BE TWO OF THEM...

...IT TAKES TWO TO TANGO.
ANOTHER GREAT FLOOD AND A KLINGON NOAH'S ARK. WHAT A WAY TO FINALLY GO...

JIM, YOU'RE GOING TO TRAVEL BACK IN TIME, PICK UP SOME WHALES, AND HOPE THEY CAN TELL THIS PROBE WHAT TO DO WITH ITSELF? IT'S INSANE!
IF YOU'VE GOT A BETTER IDEA, DOCTOR, NOW'S THE TIME--NO PUN INTENDED.

COMPUTATIONS IN PROGRESS, ADMIRAL.
EXCELLENT, SPOCK. UHURA, GET ME THROUGH TO STARFLEET COMMAND.

SIR, I'M PICKING UP A FAINT TRANSMISSION... IT'S FROM ADMIRAL KIRK!
KIRK?

STARFLEET... YOU READ?... ATTEMPT TIME TRAVEL... EXTINCT SPECIES... PROPER RESPONSE. DO... READ ME?
STABILIZE HIS SIGNAL! EMERGENCY RESERVE!

SIR, EMERGENCY POWER UNAVAILABLE--!
GOOD FORTUNE, KIRK... TO YOU, AND ALL WHO JOURNEY WITH YOU.

READY TO ENGAGE COMPUTER, ADMIRAL. WE SHOULD ARRIVE IN THE LATE 20TH CENTURY.
CAN'T YOU BE MORE SPECIFIC, MR. SPOCK?

I HAVE HAD TO PROGRAM MANY OF THE VARIABLES FROM MEMORY, ADMIRAL-- FUEL CONSUMPTION, MASS OF THIS VESSEL, THE WHALES' LOCATION...
YOU'VE PROGRAMMED THOSE FROM MEMORY?

I HAVE.
THE MEMORY OF A MAN WHOSE BRAIN WAS SCRAMBLED LIKE AN EGG! 'ANGELS AND MINISTERS OF GRACE, DEFEND US."

HAMLET.
ACT I.
SCENE 4.

MR. SPOCK, NONE OF US HAS ANY DOUBTS ABOUT YOUR MEMORY.

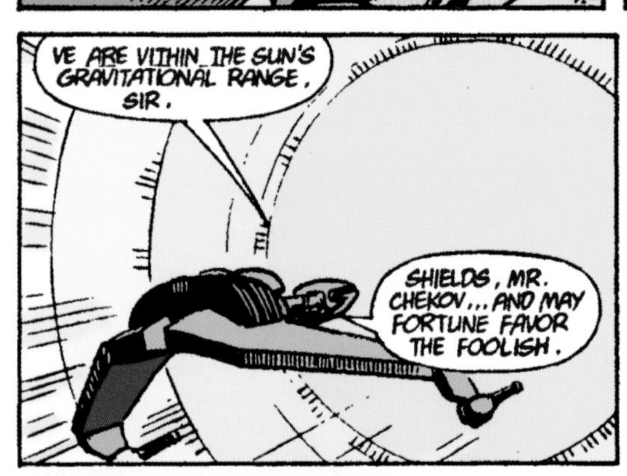
VE ARE VITHIN THE SUN'S GRAVITATIONAL RANGE, SIR.
SHIELDS, MR. CHEKOV... AND MAY FORTUNE FAVOR THE FOOLISH.

MR. SULU, WARP SPEED.
AYE, SIR...

ADMIRAL, I DON'T THINK SHE'LL HOLD TOGETHER!
IT'S TOO LATE NOW, SCOTTY...

NOW, SULU--

KRA-KOOOOM
BREAKAWAY SPEED!

UNHHHH...MIST-- MR. SULU...?

BREAKING...THRUSTERS SEEM TO HAVE FIRED, SIR...
SCREEN ON.

EARTH, ALL RIGHT...BUT WHEN? SPOCK?
JUDGING BY THE POLLUTION CONTENT OF THE ATMOSPHERE, I BELIEVE WE HAVE ARRIVED AT THE LATE 20th CENTURY.
ADMIRAL, I AM RECEIVING WHALE SONGS.

HOME IN ON THE STRONGEST SIGNAL, UHURA. DESCEND FROM ORBIT.
ADMIRAL, WE ARE CERTAINLY VISIBLE TO THE TRACKING DEVICES OF THIS ERA.
QUITE RIGHT, SPOCK. CHEKOV, ENGAGE CLOAKING DEVICE.

INDIVIDUAL WHALESONG GETTING STRONGER... ADMIRAL, IT'S COMING FROM DIRECTLY AHEAD-- FROM SAN FRANCISCO.
FROM A CITY? THAT DOESN'T MAKE SENSE...
ADMIRAL, YOU AND SPOCK HAD BETTER GET DOWN HERE... WE'VE GOT TROUBLE!

IT'S THE DILITHIUM CRYSTALS, SIR... THEY'RE GIVING OUT-- DE-CRYSTALIZING. I'D SAY WE'VE GOT 24 HOURS BEFORE WE'RE COMPLETELY POWERLESS.
WE CAN'T BE STOPPED BY THIS. ISN'T THERE ANY WAY DILITHIUM CAN BE RE-CRYSTALIZED?

SORRY, SIR. EVEN IN THE 23RD CENTURY, WE CAN'T DO THAT.
THERE IS A 20th CENTURY POSSIBILITY.
EXPLAIN.

THERE WAS A BRIEF FLIRTATION WITH NUCLEAR FISSION REACTORS IN THIS ERA. SOME SHOULD STILL BE EXTANT.
BUT HOW WOULD THAT HELP, SPOCK?

A DEVICE COULD BE FASHIONED TO COLLECT THE FISSION REACTOR'S HIGH ENERGY PHOTONS; THESE PHOTONS ARE THEORIZED TO CAUSE CRYSTALLINE RESTRUCTURING... THEORETICALLY.
WHERE WOULD WE FIND ONE OF THESE FISSION REACTORS... THEORETICALLY?

"NUCLEAR POWER WAS WIDELY USED IN NAVAL VESSELS, SUCH AS THOSE FOUND IN SAN FRANCISCO NAVAL YARD."
MR. SULU, SET US DOWN IN GOLDEN GATE PARK.
WHOOOOOOM

WE'LL DIVIDE INTO TEAMS. COMMANDERS UHURA AND CHEKOV ARE ASSIGNED TO THE FISSION REACTOR PROBLEM.
YES, SIR.

DR. McCOY, YOU, MR. SCOTT, AND COMMANDER SULU WILL PROCURE FOR US A SUITABLE WHALE TANK.
I'M A DOCTOR, NOT AN OCEANOGRAPHER!

CAPTAIN SPOCK AND I WILL ATTEMPT TO TRACE THESE WHALE SONGS TO THEIR SOURCE.
I WANT YOU ALL TO BE VERY CAREFUL. FROM VISITING THIS ERA BEFORE, WE KNOW IT TO BE AN EXTREMELY PRIMITIVE AND PARANOID CULTURE. THESE PEOPLE HAVE NEVER SEEN AN EXTRATERRESTRIAL BEFORE.

VERY GOOD, MR. SPOCK.

EVERYONE REMEMBER WHERE WE PARKED.

SPREAD OUT, ALL OF YOU... TRY NOT TO LOOK CONSPICUOUS.
DELI

DAMN, THEY'RE STILL USING MONEY... WE'RE GOING TO NEED SOME. SPOCK, YOU COME WITH ME.
ANTIQUES
WE BUY AND SELL

SUTTON'S
JOKEY CLUB
SREEEEEEE
WATCH WHERE YOU'RE GOING, YOU DUMB ASS!

AND A...
...A...
...A DOUBLE DUMB ASS TO YOU!
MOTINS

ADMIRAL, YOUR USE OF PROFANITY--
IT'S SIMPLY THE WAY THEY TALK, SPOCK.
AND CALL ME "JIM".

YES, THEY'RE 18th CENTURY AMERICAN... QUITE VALUABLE...

...YOU'RE SURE YOU WANT TO PART WITH THEM?
HOW MUCH WILL YOU GIVE ME?

ADMIRAL, THOSE WERE A BIRTHDAY PRESENT FROM DR. McCOY.
AND THEY WILL BE AGAIN, SPOCK; THAT'S THE BEAUTY OF IT.

I'LL GIVE YOU 200 BUCKS, TAKE IT OR LEAVE IT.
I'LL TAKE IT.
IS THAT A LOT?

THIS MAY NOT BE A LOT OF MONEY, BUT IT'S ALL WE HAVE, SO NOBODY SPLURGE. GOOD HUNTING.

CITY MAP
A JUXTAPOSING OF OUR COORDINATES WITH THIS MAP SHOULD SHOW US WHERE THE WHALES ARE LOCATED.
NO, SPOCK, I THINK WE'LL FIND WHAT WE'RE LOOKING FOR AT THE CETACEAN INSTITUTE IN SAUSALITO. TWO HUMPBACKS CALLED GEORGE AND GRACIE.

MAP
HOW DO YOU KNOW THIS?
SEE GEORGE AND GRACIE THE ONLY HUMPBACK WHALES IN CAPTIVITY- AT THE CETACEAN INSTITUTE, SAUSAL
SIMPLE LOGIC.

ADMIRAL, IS THE TERM "EXACT CHANGE" ANOTHER FORM OF PROFANITY?

TEAM LEADER, THIS IS TEAM 2. COME IN, PLEASE...

TEAM 2, KIRK HERE.
ADMIRAL, WE HAVE FOUND THE NUCLEAR WESSEL. WE WILL BEAM IN TONIGHT, COLLECT THE PHOTONS AND BE GONE BEFORE ANYONE SUSPECTS.

WELL DONE, CHEKOV.
USS ENTERPRISE CVN 65
AND ADMIRAL, YOU'LL NEVER GUESS WHICH WESSEL IT IS...

CHEKOV AND UHURA HAVE FOUND--
EXCUSE ME, ADMIRAL?

EXCUSE ME, COULD YOU PLEASE TURN THAT THING--

--DOWN?

CLAP CLAP CLAP CLAP
AS YOU OBSERVED, A PRIMITIVE CULTURE.
CETACEAN INSTITUTE, SAUSALITO.

CETACEAN INSTITUTE
MY NAME'S DR. GILLIAN TAYLOR, BUT YOU CAN CALL ME GILLIAN. I'LL BE YOUR GUIDE THIS MORNING. FIRST, I'D LIKE TO INTRODUCE YOU TO THE INSTITUTE'S PRIDE AND JOY...

"...THE ONLY TWO HUMPBACK WHALES IN CAPTIVITY, GEORGE AND GRACIE. THEY WEIGH 45,000 POUNDS EACH..."

IT'S PERFECT, SPOCK, A MALE AND A FEMALE. WE CAN BEAM THEM UP AND CONSIDER OURSELVES DAMN LUCKY.
NOW IF YOU'LL FOLLOW ME...

...HERE'S A MUCH BETTER WAY TO SEE THEM-- UNDERWATER. TAKE A GOOD LOOK, BECAUSE SOON WE'LL BE SENDING THEM BACK TO THE OCEAN.
SPOCK?

REEEEKTT-REEEEKKT
WHAT YOU'RE HEARING IS THE WHALESONG, SUNG BY THE MALE. WE STILL DON'T KNOW WHAT PURPOSE THE SONGS SERVE.
MAYBE HE'S SINGING TO THE MAN.

MAN? WHAT--
WHAT THE HELL? EXCUSE ME!

WHO THE HELL ARE YOU? WHAT THE HELL WERE YOU DOING IN THERE?
HE DIDN'T MEAN ANY HARM, I ASSURE--

I WAS... ATTEMPTING THE HELL TO COMMUNICATE.

OH, YOU WERE? WELL, I WANT YOU GUYS THE HELL OUT OF HERE, RIGHT NOW...

"...OR I CALL THE COPS!"
SPOCK, DON'T TRY USING PROFANITY LIKE THE LOCALS. YOU HAVEN'T QUITE GOT THE HANG OF IT YET.
UNDERSTOOD, ADMIRAL.

DID YOU LEARN ANYTHING FROM YOUR MIND MELD?
THE WHALES ARE VERY UNHAPPY ABOUT THE WAY THEIR SPECIES HAS BEEN TREATED BY MAN.

THEY HAVE A RIGHT TO BE. DID THEY UNDERSTAND YOU? DO YOU THINK THEY'LL HELP US?
I BELIEVE I WAS SUCCESSFUL IN COMMUNICATING OUR INTENTIONS.

IT'S ALL RIGHT, THEY DIDN'T MEAN ANY HARM...
GILLIAN, I HEARD THERE WAS SOME EXCITEMENT.
REEEEKT-T
REEEEKKT

IT WAS NOTHING, BOB. JUST A COUPLE OF KOOKS. THEY'RE OKAY.
BUT YOU'RE NOT, I CAN TELL. I'VE KNOWN YOU TOO LONG.

BOB...IT'S TEARING ME APART... TO HAVE TO SEND THEM BACK INTO THE OCEAN...
WE CAN'T AFFORD TO EVEN FEED THEM, KIDDO. IT'S NOT FAIR TO THEM.

AND AFTER ALL, IT'S NOT LIKE THEY'RE HUMAN BEINGS. THEIR INTELLIGENCE HAS IN NO WAY BEEN PROVEN COMPARABLE TO OURS--
I DON'T KNOW ABOUT YOU, BUT MY COMPASSION FOR SOMEONE IS NOT LIMITED TO MY ESTIMATE OF THEIR INTELLIGENCE!

WE ALL SQUARED AWAY, JOE?
YEAH, DR. BRIGGS... BUT DR. TAYLOR'S GONNA GO BERSERK.

IT'S THE ONLY WAY, JOE. SHE'LL CALL ME NAMES FOR AWHILE, BUT THEN SHE'LL UNDERSTAND.
AFTER ALL, IT'S FOR HER OWN GOOD.

WELL, WELL!

WALKING? I THOUGHT YOU'D BE TAKING THE WHALE EXPRESS BACK HOME.
THERE'S REALLY VERY LITTLE POINT IN MY TRYING TO EXPLAIN.

I'LL BUY THAT. C'MON, LET ME GIVE YOU A LIFT. I HAVE A NOTORIOUS WEAKNESS FOR HARD LUCK CASES.
WE DON'T WANT TO BE ANY TROUBLE.

YOU'VE ALREADY BEEN THAT...

...BESIDES, I WANT TO KNOW WHAT YOU WERE REALLY TRYING TO DO BACK THERE. WAS IT SOME KIND OF MACHO THING, OR WHAT?
CAN I ASK YOU SOMETHING?

WHAT'S GOING TO HAPPEN TO THE WHALES WHEN YOU RELEASE THEM?
YOU'RE NOT FROM THE MILITARY, ARE YOU? TRYING TO TRAIN WHALES TO RETRIEVE TORPEDOES, OR SOMETHING LIKE THAT?

NO, IT'S NOTHING LIKE--
GRACIE IS PREGNANT.

WHAT? HOW CAN YOU KNOW THAT?
WE KNOW LOTS OF THINGS, GILLIAN... AND WE CAN HELP YOU... IN WAYS THAT, FRANKLY, YOU COULDN'T POSSIBLY IMAGINE.

YOU KNOW, I'VE GOT A HUNCH WE'D ALL BE A LOT HAPPIER TALKING OVER DINNER. WHAT DO YOU SAY?
MAYBE... YOU GUYS LIKE ITALIAN FOOD?

YES.
NO.
SIGH

PLEXICORP
WHERE THE FUTURE IS PLASTICS.
WELL, SO MUCH FOR THE TOUR OF OUR HUMBLE PLANT. I MUST SAY, PROFESSOR...

...YOUR KNOWLEDGE OF ENGINEERING IS MOST IMPRESSIVE.
BACK HOME, WE CALL "PROFESSOR SCOTT" THE MIRACLE WORKER.

IS THAT RIGHT? WELL, MAY I OFFER YOU GENTLEMEN ANYTHING?

DR. NICHOLS, I MIGHT HAVE SOMETHIN' TO OFFER YOU. I NOTICE YOU'RE STILL WORKIN' WITH POLYMERS.
"STILL"? WHAT ELSE WOULD I BE WORKING WITH?

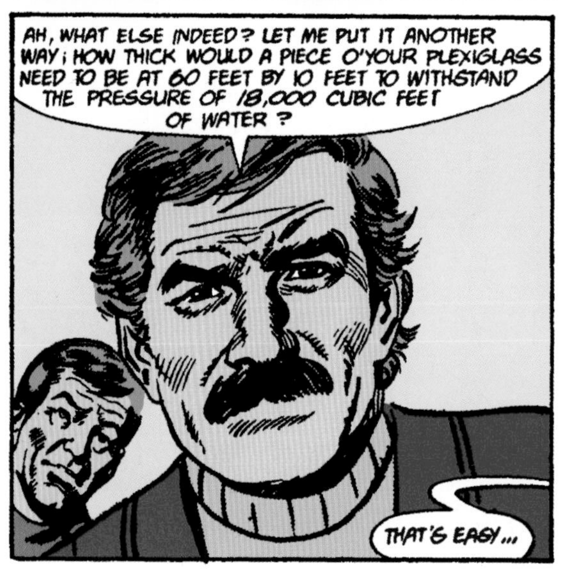
AH, WHAT ELSE INDEED? LET ME PUT IT ANOTHER WAY; HOW THICK WOULD A PIECE O'YOUR PLEXIGLASS NEED TO BE AT 60 FEET BY 10 FEET TO WITHSTAND THE PRESSURE OF 18,000 CUBIC FEET OF WATER?
THAT'S EASY...

...6 INCHES THICK. WE CARRY STUFF THAT BIG IN STOCK.
YES, BUT SUPPOSE -- JUST SUPPOSE -- I COULD SHOW YOU A WAY T' MANUFACTURE A WALL THAT WOULD DO THE SAME JOB...
...BUT WAS ONLY ONE INCH THICK. THAT'D BE WORTH SOMETHIN' T'YOU, EH?

...ARE YOU JOKING?
THE PROFESSOR NEVER JOKES. PERHAPS HE COULD USE YOUR COMPUTER...
COMPUTER--

JUST USE THE KEYBOARD, PROFESSOR.
AH, A KEYBOARD... HOW QUAINT...
KLIKA TIKKA TIKKA

INCREDIBLE... THIS MATRIX YIELDS... TRANSPARENT ALUMINUM?
YOU'LL BE RICH BEYOND THE DREAMS OF AVARICE.
WHY DON'T YOU THINK IT OVER FOR A MINUTE, LAD?

YOU KNOW, IF WE GIVE HIM THE FORMULA, WE'LL BE ALTERING THE FUTURE.
WHY? HOW DO YOU KNOW HE DINNA INVENT THE THING?

HOW DO YOU KNOW GRACIE'S PREGNANT? NOBODY KNOWS THAT.
GRACIE DOES.

I'LL BE RIGHT HERE, ADMIRAL.
SEE YOU LATER, OLD FRIEND.

"IS YOUR FRIEND JUST GOING TO HANG AROUND THE PARK WHILE WE EAT?"

"I'M SURE HE'LL FIND A WAY TO KEEP HIMSELF OCCUPIED..."
HMMMMNNNNNN

YOU KNOW, GILLIAN, I COULD TAKE THOSE WHALES SOMEPLACE WHERE THEY WOULDN'T BE HUNTED.
YOU? YOU CAN'T EVEN GET FROM SAUSALITO TO SAN FRANCISCO WITHOUT A LIFT.

WHERE WOULD YOU TAKE THEM?
IT'S NOT SO MUCH A MATTER OF PLACE AS A MATTER OF TIME...

WHO ARE YOU, ANYWAY? YOU TALK LIKE YOU'RE FROM OUTER SPACE.
NO, I'M FROM IOWA. I JUST WORK IN OUTER SPACE.

YOU WANT THE TRUTH? I'M FROM THE 23RD CENTURY. I'VE BEEN SENT HERE TO BRING BACK TWO HUMPBACK WHALES TO... REPOPULATE THE SPECIES.
WELL, YOUR FRIEND WAS RIGHT. GRACIE IS VERY PREGNANT. SHE AND GEORGE ARE BEING SHIPPED OUT AT NOON TOMORROW.

NOON? COME ON, I DON'T HAVE MUCH TIME.
JUST PUT IT ON MY BILL...

USS ENTERPRISE CVN 65

HMMMMMMMMMMMMMMM

REACTOR ROOM
AUTHORIZED PERSONNEL ONLY
THIS WAY, UHURA.
BREAK OUT THE COLLECTING DEVICE.

HOW LONG WILL IT TAKE?
WITH THIS TECHNOLOGY? NO WAY OF TELLING...

REACTOR ROOM
SECURITY CLEARANCE ONLY
...DEPENDS ON HOW MUCH SHIELDING IS BETWEEN US AND THE REACTOR.

YES, WE'RE GOING TO TAG GEORGE AND GRACIE WITH RADIO TRANSMITTERS, SO WE CAN KEEP TABS ON THEM--IF THE DAMN HUNTERS DON'T GET THEM FIRST--
--BUT I CAN'T TELL YOU THE FREQUENCY! IT'S CLASSIFIED!
ALL RIGHT, GILLIAN. BUT I'M HERE TO TAKE TWO HUMPBACK WHALES TO THE 23RD CENTURY. ANY TWO...

... BUT I'D JUST AS SOON TAKE YOURS. BETTER FOR *THEM*, BETTER FOR *ME*, AND BETTER FOR *YOU*.
I BET YOU'RE A DAMN GOOD POKER PLAYER.

THE BEST.

THINK ABOUT IT... BUT DON'T TAKE *TOO* LONG. IF YOU CHANGE YOUR MIND, THIS IS WHERE I'LL BE.
HERE? IN THE PARK?
HERE.

?
HMMMMMMMMMMMMMM

KIRK...?
AAMMMMMNNNNNNN

STATUS?
THE WHALE TANK WILL BE FINISHED BY MORNING, ADMIRAL; WE HAVE NO WORD FROM UHURA AND CHEKOV SINCE BEAM-IN.

DAMN. WE'VE BEEN SO LUCKY... WE HAVE THE TWO PERFECT WHALES IN OUR HANDS, BUT IF WE DON'T MOVE QUICKLY, WE'LL LOSE THEM!
IN THAT EVENT, THE PROBABILITIES ARE THAT OUR MISSION WOULD FAIL.

OUR MISSION?! GOD DAMN IT, SPOCK, YOU'RE TALKING ABOUT THE LIVES OF EVERY HUMAN ON EARTH!
YOU'RE HALF-HUMAN, HAVEN'T YOU GOT ANY FEELINGS ABOUT THAT?

I...
...I DO NOT UNDERSTAND.

YES, CHIEF. WE'RE PICKING UP THE INTERFERENCE DOWN HERE, TOO. WHAT DO YOU MAKE OF IT?
YES, I AGREE.

ALERT SECURITY-- WE HAVE AN INTRUDER IN THE REACTOR ROOM.
YESSIR!

UHURA TO MR. SCOTT... COME IN, SCOTTY...
IT'S FINISHED.

AYE, LASS, I HEAR YOU. MY POWER'S MINIMAL, SO I'LL HAVE T'BRING YOU IN ONE AT A TIME...

...STAND BY...
STANDING BY, MR. SCOTT... HOW SOON?

SCOTTY? NOW VOULD BE A GOOD TIME TO--
FREEZE!

CERTAINLY. BUT, COULD YOU TELL ME...
PRECISELY VHAT DOES THAT MEAN-- "FREEZE"?

SECURITY
ALL RIGHT, "COMMANDER," LET'S TAKE IT FROM THE TOP.

=SIGH= I HAVE TOLD YOU. I AM LT. COMMANDER PAVEL CHEKOV, IN STARFLEET, UNITED FEDERATION OF PLANETS, SERVICE NUMBER 656-58273
WHAT DO YOU THINK?
I THINK HE'S A RUSSKIE...

NO KIDDING.
...BUT I ALSO THINK HE'S A RETARD OR SOMETHING. LET'S HAND THIS ONE OVER TO WASHING--
DO NOT MOVE.

GIVE US THE RAY GUN, PAL.
I VARN YOU. LIE ON THE FLOOR, OR I VILL HAVE TO STUN YOU.

GO AHEAD. STUN ME.
I'M WERY SORRY, BUT--

IT MUST HAVE BEEN THE RADIATION...

BETTER SOUND A GENERAL ALARM, BUT TELL THEM TO GO EASY ON HIM.

AOOGAH AOOGAH
VUN LEAP AND I AM HOME FR--

DAMN-- SOMEBODY GET AN AMBULANCE.

ANY LUCK?
NOTHING ON ANY OF THE EMERGENCY STATIONS...

...I NEVER SHOULD HAVE LEFT HIM...
I UNDERSTAND HOW YOU FEEL, UHURA, BUT IT WAS NECESSARY.
KEEP TRYING. YOU'LL FIND HIM.

MR. SCOTT, YOU PROMISED ME AN ESTIMATE ON THE DILITHIUM CRYSTALS...
IT'S SLOW GOIN', SIR. IT'LL BE WELL INTO TOMORROW.

NOT GOOD ENOUGH, SCOTTY. YOU'VE GOT TO DO BETTER. KLIK
HE'S GOT HIMSELF IN A BIT OF A SNIT, DON'T HE.

HE IS A MAN OF DEEP... FEELINGS.

? NO PRESS CREWS... WHAT'S GOING ON HERE...?
CETACEAN INSTITUTE

GEORGE...GRACIE--
THEY'RE GONE!
HOW--?
THEY LEFT LAST NIGHT, GILLIAN.

BOB--?
WE DIDN'T WANT A MOB SCENE WITH THE PRESS... AND I THOUGHT IT WOULD BE EASIER ON YOU THIS WAY.

YOU JUST--JUST SENT THEM AWAY?
WITHOUT EVEN LETTING ME SAY GOODBYE?
GILLIAN, TRY TO--

KRAKT
YOU SON OF A BITCH!

KIRK?
SCREEEECH

KIRK, WHERE ARE YOU? KIRK!
?
WHUPWHUPWHUP

AND I THOUGHT THE *BIRD OF PREY* HANDLED LIKE A GARBAGE SCOW...!

FLEXICORP
WHAT'S HE DOING...?

SULU TO SCOTTY, LOWERING TRANSPARENT ALUMINUM.
AYE, LAD, JUST WHAT THE DOCTOR ORDERED.

CLUNK
THERE MUST BE SOMETHING *HERE*, EVEN IF I CAN'T *SEE* IT! BUT WHERE--
OW!

ADMIRAL, WE HAVE A PROBLEM.
=SIGH= KIRK TO TRANSPORTER ROOM...
KIRK? KIRK!!

WHAT--?
HMMMMMMMMM

HELLO, ALICE...

...WELCOME TO WONDERLAND.

IT'S TRUE... WHAT YOU SAID...
EVERY WORD. STEADY NOW, WE NEED YOUR HELP.

SEE ? THE STORAGE TANKS FOR THE WHALES. WE'LL BRING THEM UP JUST LIKE WE BROUGHT YOU...
KIRK, THEY'RE GONE. THEY WERE TAKEN LAST NIGHT. THEY COULD BE IN ALASKA BY NOW!

...BUT THEY'RE TAGGED, WITH RADIO TRANSMITTERS. CAN'T YOU FIND THEM ?
AT THE MOMENT, WE CAN'T GO ANYWHERE.

WHAT KIND OF SPACESHIP IS THIS, ANYWAY?
A SPACESHIP WITH A MISSING MAN.

ADMIRAL, FULL POWER IS RESTORED.
THANK YOU, SPOCK.

HELLO, DOCTOR TAYLOR. WELCOME ABOARD.
...IF I'M ALICE...YOU MUST BE THE WHITE RABBIT, RIGHT?
YOU'RE NOT FAR WRONG.

ADMIRAL...I'VE FOUND CHEKOV, SIR. HE...HE'S IN EMERGENCY SURGERY, RIGHT NOW.
WHERE?

...MERCY HOSPITAL.
JIM, YOU'VE GOT TO LET ME GO! DON'T LEAVE HIM IN THE HANDS OF 20th CENTURY MEDICINE!

WHAT DO YOU THINK, SPOCK?
ADMIRAL, DR. McCOY IS CORRECT. WE MUST HELP COMMANDER CHEKOV.

IS THAT THE LOGICAL THING TO DO, SPOCK?
NO, ADMIRAL... BUT IT IS THE HUMAN THING TO DO. THE NEEDS OF THE ONE OUTWEIGH THE NEEDS OF THE MANY.

RIGHT.
WILL YOU HELP US?
SURE, BUT... HOW?

"...WE'LL NEED TO LOOK LIKE PHYSICIANS..."
I'LL CHECK THE REGISTRY, YOU WAIT HERE.

HIS CONDITION IS CRITICAL. THEY'RE HOLDING HIM IN A SECURITY WARD, ONE FLIGHT UP.
SECURITY WARD? HOW'LL WE GET TO HIM?

I THINK I CAN FILL THAT PRESCRIPTION, COLLEAGUES. COME ON.
WARD

ONE SIDE, PLEASE.
SECURITY WARD
SORRY, DOC...

...WE HAVE STRICT ORDERS. NO ONE GOES IN HERE.
DAMMIT, ALL THE OTHER OPERATING ROOMS ARE OCCUPIED!
THIS IS AN EMERGENCY!

THIS WOMAN HAS IMMEDIATE POST PRANDIAL UPPER ABDOMINAL DISTENSION! DO YOU WANT HER DEATH ON YOUR CONSCIENCE?
AAAGGGN!

OKAY, DOC, GO AHEAD.
ABOUT TIME.

WHAT DID YOU SAY SHE HAS?
CRAMPS.

WHO ARE YOU? DOCTOR ADAMS WAS SUPPOSED TO ASSIST ME.
WE'RE JUST OBSERVING.

WHAT THE HELL DO YOU THINK YOU'RE DOING?
IT'S AN EXPERIMENTAL DEVICE, DOCTOR.
...TEARING OF THE MIDDLE MENINGEAL ARTERY...
eeeeeeeeeeeee

THIS IS MY PATIENT, AND I'M PERFORMING THE OPERATION!
OPERATION? MY GOD, MAN, DO YOU PLAN TO CARVE HIM OPEN LIKE A TURKEY?

A SIMPLE EVACUATION OF THE EXPANDING EPIDURAL HEMATOME WILL RELIEVE THE PRESSURE!
DRILLING HOLES IN HIS HEAD IS NOT THE ANSWER! HIS ARTERY MUST BE REPAIRED! PUT AWAY YOUR BUTCHER KNIVES AND LET ME SAVE THE PATIENT!

I DON'T KNOW WHO THE HELL YOU ARE, BUT I'M GOING TO HAVE YOU REMOVED.
DOCTORS, DOCTORS, THIS IS HIGHLY UNPROFESSIONAL--

--WHY NOT CALM DOWN AND THINK IT OVER?
CHOPT
UNH

EVERYONE, INTO THAT STOREROOM BEHIND YOU, AND NO ONE WILL BE HURT.
DO AS HE SAYS.
GASP

HOW IS HE, BONES?
I GOT TO HIM JUST IN TIME, JIM... BLASTED BUTCHERS... HE SHOULD BE UP AND AROUND ANY MOMENT NOW.
MMMmmmm

UNHHHH...
PAVEL, CAN YOU HEAR ME? GIVE ME YOUR NAME AND RANK.

NAME--CHEKOV, PAVEL A..., RANK--
...ADMIRAL...

DON'T YOU GUYS HAVE ANY ENLISTED TYPES...?

HOW'S THE PATIENT?
HE'S GOING TO MAKE IT, THANKS.

"HE"...?
THEY WENT IN WITH A SHE...
STOP!

REAL PHYSICIANS DO NOT FORGET THEIR PATIENT'S GENDER, ADMIRAL!
ONE LITTLE MISTAKE...

IT'S WORKIN', MR. SPOCK! THE CRYSTALS ARE REENERGIZIN'!
I AM CAPABLE OF SEEING THAT MYSELF, MR. SCOTT...

"...I WONDER, HOWEVER, WHAT IS DELAYING THE ADMIRAL AND HIS PARTY."
STOP! STOP, OR WE'LL SHOOT!

ELEVATOR
IN HERE-- QUICKLY!
BUT KIRK...!

ELEVATOR
WE'VE GOT 'EM! THEY'RE IN THE ELEVATOR, ON THEIR WAY DOWN TO YOU!
ROGER, SERGEANT...

ELEVATOR
...WE'LL TAKE CARE OF THEM.
HMMMMMMMM
WHAT'S THAT SOUND...?

ELEVATOR
WHERE... WHERE'D THEY GO?

I TOLD YOU, KIRK--I'M COMING WITH YOU!
GILLIAN, THAT'S IMPOSSIBLE. JUST GIVE ME THE FREQUENCY OF THE WHALES' TRANSMITTERS.

≡SIGH≡ I GUESS YOU'RE RIGHT. THE FREQUENCY IS 401 MEGAHERTZ.
THANK YOU... FOR EVERYTHING.
BEAM ME UP, SCOTTY.

YOU'VE GOT A STOWAWAY, ADMIRAL!
HMMMMMMM

YOU TRICKED ME.
YOU NEED ME. AND BESIDES, I'VE GOT NOBODY BUT THOSE WHALES. I'M GOING TO MAKE SURE THEY'RE SAFE.

ALL RIGHT, GILLIAN.
MR. SPOCK, WHERE THE HELL IS THE POWER YOU PROMISED ME?
ADMIRAL, YOU MUST WAIT ONE DAMN MINUTE.

SCOTT HERE, SIR. LET'S GO FIND THEM WHALES!
MR. SULU?
THIS THING LOOKS PRETTY GOOD AFTER A HELICOPTER...

"GO, MR. SULU."
WHOOOOOM

YOU PRESENT THE APPEARANCE OF A MAN WITH A PROBLEM, SPOCK.
YES, DOCTOR. TO RETURN US TO THE 23RD CENTURY, I HAVE USED OUR JOURNEY BACK AS A REFERENT, CALCULATING THE COEFFICIENT OF ELAPSED TIME IN RELATION TO THE ACCELERATION CURVE.

UH... NATURALLY.
SO WHAT'S YOUR PROBLEM?
WITH THE WEIGHT OF THE WHALES ADDED, ACCELERATION IS NO LONGER A CONSTANT.

WELL, YOU'RE JUST GOING TO HAVE TO TAKE YOUR BEST SHOT. A GUESS, SPOCK. YOUR BEST GUESS.
DOCTOR, "GUESSING" IS NOT IN MY NATURE.

WELL, NOBODY'S PERFECT.

ADMIRAL, I HAVE CONTACT WITH THE WHALES, BUT THERE'S ANOTHER VESSEL IN THE VICINITY, CLOSING IN ON THEM.
ON SCREEN.

OH MY GOD--THAT'S A WHALING SHIP!

"MR. SULU, FULL POWER DESCENT-- ACTIVATE CLOAKING DEVICE!"

"THE WHALING SHIP IS ONE NAUTICAL MILE FROM THE WHALES, SIR."

FULL POWER DESCENT, MR. SULU. ON MY COMMAND.

"DISENGAGE CLOAKING DEVICE!"
KA-TWANNG

MR. SCOTT, IT'S UP TO YOU NOW.
ENERGIZE.
I'LL GIVE IT ME BEST, SIR.

STAY WITH ME, GIRL... YOU CAN DO IT...

ADMIRAL! THERE BE WHALES HERE!
WELL DONE, MR. SCOTT. WARP SPEED AS SOON AS POSSIBLE.

AYE, SIR--WARP SPEED!
KA-WHOOOM

MR. SPOCK, HAVE YOU ACCOUNTED FOR THE VARIABLE MASS OF WHALES AND WATER IN YOUR TIME RE-ENTRY PROGRAM?
MR. SCOTT CANNOT GIVE ME EXACT FIGURES, ADMIRAL. I WILL THERE-FORE...
...MAKE A GUESS.

YOU? SPOCK, THAT'S EXTRAORDINARY.
WELCOME BACK.
?

IRONIC. WHEN MAN WAS KILLING THESE CREATURES, HE WAS DESTROYING HIS OWN FUTURE.
IT'S A MIRACLE, MR. SCOTT.
NO, LASS...

"...THE MIRACLE IS YET TO COME."
WARP 7.9... MR. SULU, THAT'S ALL I CAN GIVE YE!
SHIELDS AT MAXIMUM!

CAN WE MAKE BREAKAWAY SPEED?
ADMIRAL, I CANNOT EVEN GUARANTEE WE WILL ESCAPE THE SUN'S GRAVITY. I WILL ATTEMPT TO COMPENSATE BY ALTERING OUR TRAJECTORY.

ACCELERATION THRUSTER AT SPOCK'S COMMAND...!

STEADY...
...STEADY...
KRA-KOOOOM
...NOW.

...DID... DID BREAKING THRUSTERS FIRE?
THEY DID, ADMIRAL.

ADMIRAL, I'VE GOT THAT STRANGE INTERFERENCE, AS BEFORE.
SIR, I HAVE NO CONTROL! WE'VE LOST ALL POWER!
MRRRAAAWWNKKH

OUT OF CONTROL, BONES, AND BLIND AS A BAT!
FOR GOD'S SAKE, JIM, WHERE ARE WE?

WHAPPT

BLOW THE HATCH, SPOCK!
FOOMPT

YOU GOT US HOME, SPOCK, NOW ALL WE HAVE TO DO IS FREE THE *WHALES*! SEE TO THE SAFETY OF ALL HANDS.
UNDERSTOOD, ADMIRAL.

DAMN SALT WATER'S JAMMED THE BLOODY *DOOR*...!

EASY, SCOTTY-- THE EMERGENCY RELEASE STILL WORKS! WHAT ABOUT THE WHALES?
I CANNA RELEASE THEM, ADMIRAL-- NO POWER TO THE BAY DOORS!

WE'LL HAVE TO USE THE EXPLOSIVE OVERRIDE!
ADMIRAL, *DON'T*--IF THIS BUCKET OF BOLTS GOES DOWN, YOU'LL BE *TRAPPED*!

WHERE IS THE ADMIRAL?
HE'S GONE BACK T'FREE THE WHALES.
I HOPE HE DOESN'T GO DOWN WITH THE SHIP!
CARGO BAY OVERRIDE
GASPE
KIRK--!

ARE YOU OKAY? ARE THE WHALES --
I RELEASED THEM. WHY DON'T THEY ANSWER?
"DAMN IT. WHY DON'T THEY SING?"
MRRRAAAWWKK
REEEKKT-REEEKKT
MRRAWWK
REEEKKT-REEEKKT

REEEKKT. REEEKKKT
SPACEDOCK TO STARFLEET COMMAND, WE ARE OPERATIONAL AGAIN. DO YOU READ, STARFLEET...?

MR. PRESIDENT, WE HAVE POWER!
BY GOD! LAUNCH RESCUE SHUTTLE!

WHO WERE THEY, JIM? WHAT DID THEY WANT?
WE'LL NEVER KNOW, BONES...

"...BUT I REMEMBER A VERY OLD STORY. AND I THINK WE'VE BEEN GIVEN A SECOND-- NO, A THIRD CHANCE."

REEEKKT. REEEKKT

CAPTAIN SPOCK, YOU DO NOT STAND ACCUSED.
I REALIZE THAT, MR. PRESIDENT...

...HOWEVER, I STAND WITH MY SHIPMATES. THEIR FATE SHALL BE MINE.
AS YOU WISH. ADMIRAL KIRK, YOU HAVE HEARD THE SEVERAL COUNTS OF CONSPIRACY, ASSAULT, THEFT, SABOTAGE, WILLFUL DESTRUCTION AND MUTINY. HOW DO YOU PLEAD?

ON BEHALF OF US ALL, MR. PRESIDENT, I PLEAD GUILTY.
SO ENTERED. HOWEVER, BECAUSE OF CERTAIN =AHEM= MITIGATING CIRCUMSTANCES, ALL CHARGES BUT ONE ARE SUMMARILY DISMISSED.
THE REMAINING CHARGE, DISOBEYING A SUPERIOR OFFICER, IS DIRECTED ONLY AT ADMIRAL KIRK.

JAMES T. KIRK, IT IS THE JUDGMENT OF THIS COUNCIL THAT YOU BE REDUCED IN RANK TO CAPTAIN...

...AND THAT, AS A CONSEQUENCE OF YOUR NEW RANK, YOU BE GIVEN THE DUTIES FOR WHICH YOU HAVE REPEATEDLY DEMONSTRATED UNSWERVING ABILITY:
THE COMMAND OF A STARSHIP.

CAPTAIN KIRK, YOUR NEW COMMAND AWAITS YOU. YOU AND YOUR CREW HAVE SAVED THIS PLANET FROM ITS OWN SHORTSIGHTEDNESS...
...AND WE ARE FOREVER IN YOUR DEBT.
YAYYYY

CONGRATULATIONS, KIRK. THEY PUT ME ON A SHIP, TOO--A SCIENCE VESSEL. I'VE GOT 300 YEARS OF CATCH-UP LEARNING TO DO.
YOU MEAN THIS IS GOODBYE?

NOT YET. DON'T WORRY, I'LL FIND YOU!
SEE YOU AROUND-- THE GALAXY.

I WILL BE RETURNING TO VULCAN WITHIN THE HOUR. I WISHED TO TAKE MY LEAVE OF YOU.
IT IS KIND OF YOU TO MAKE THIS EFFORT.

IT IS NOT AN EFFORT. YOU ARE MY SON. AS I RECALL, I OPPOSED YOUR ENLISTMENT IN STARFLEET. IT IS POSSIBLE MY JUDGMENT WAS INCORRECT.
YOUR ASSOCIATES ARE PEOPLE OF GOOD CHARACTER.
THEY ARE MY FRIENDS.

YES, OF COURSE. DO YOU HAVE ANY MESSAGE FOR YOUR MOTHER?
TELL HER...

TELL HER I FEEL FINE.
UNDERSTOOD.

THE BUREAUCRATIC MENTALITY IS THE ONLY CONSTANT IN THE UNIVERSE. WE'LL GET A FREIGHTER.
WITH ALL RESPECT, DOC, I'M COUNTING ON EXCELSIOR.
EXCELSIOR? SULU, WHY IN GOD'S NAME WOULD YOU WANT THAT BUCKET O'BOLTS?
SCOTTY, DON'T PREJUDGE. A SHIP IS A SHIP.
JIM, LOOK!
NCC-1701-A

WHAT IN BLAZES--?
LOGICAL.
MY FRIENDS...
"...WE'VE COME HOME."

SPACE, THE FINAL FRONTIER.
TO YOUR POSTS, GENTLEMEN.
THESE ARE THE VOYAGES OF THE STARSHIP ENTERPRISE.

HER ONGOING MISSION: TO EXPLORE STRANGE NEW WORLDS,
LET'S SEE WHAT SHE'S GOT, MR. SULU. AHEAD WARP FACTOR ONE.
AYE, SIR; WARP FACTOR ONE.
TO SEEK OUT NEW LIFE AND NEW CIVILIZATIONS,

TO BOLDLY GO WHERE NO MAN HAS GONE BEFORE.
AND THE ADVENTURE CONTINUES...
THE END

ART BY DAVID DIETRICK

STAR TREK®

MOTION PICTURE TRILOGY